CAMP TALLAWANDA

CAMP TALLAWANDA

MICHAEL DAVE

For my Family and Friends

CHAPTER 1

Everybody Goes to Camp Tallawanda

"You were already on summer break?" TJ Stanton asked with his head thrust forward. "And you're coming back to school?"

Ricky Collins shifted his thumbs from underneath his backpack straps and sighed, "Yup."

They walked side by side to their last day of school before summer. Eager students flooded the sidewalk hurrying to get to school so that it would be over and done with for the year. TJ didn't bother wearing his backpack.

"So, you finished sixth grade?" TJ recapped the explanation Ricky had just given. "But your parents told you to come to school with me? On the last day! Cause they wanted to be good next-door neighbors?"

"And we're the same age," Ricky added.

"Why would they make you come for one day?" TJ couldn't wrap his mind around it.

"I don't know," Ricky groaned. "They said it'd help me make friends before starting seventh grade, or something."

"Your parents moved you across the country before the last day of sixth grade, and actually think you'd make friends before starting junior high next year?"

Ricky let out another deflated exhale, "I guess."

TJ shook his head, "Are they nuts?"

The boys rounded the corner where the long red-bricked school sat waiting for them. Two large cement columns stood at the sliding door entrance. Freshly trimmed grass covered the front lawn, its corners lined-up perfectly with the sidewalks. Girls and boys ran around with the pure joy of freedom knowing summer was only a few agonizing hours away.

"This is a lot nicer than my old school," Ricky said.

"The junior high is even better, just wait till next year," TJ assured his new neighbor.

"Well, I think this is still pretty neat."

"*Neat*?" TJ mocked. "What are your parents thinking?"

"I told you, they wanted me to make friends."

"How do they figure a kid who says *neat* and shows up a day before summer is going to make friends?"

Ricky thought about it for a while, "At lunch?" he suggested.

"Dude, you're in for a rude awakening. Moving in on the last day like this, and starting junior high with no friends?" TJ exhaled. "It's a social death sentence."

Ricky lowered his eyes to the ground.

"But," TJ stopped, waiting until Ricky looked back at him. "Don't worry, man. There's a perfect solution," TJ smiled.

"There is?"

"If you want to make friends before starting junior high, you need to come to Camp Tallawanda," TJ explained.

"Camp Tall-what?"

"Ta-la-wan-duh. Every kid in town goes. And it's the best place on the whole planet," TJ said with his brown eyes wide open. "You want any friends before going to junior high?"

Ricky nodded.

"Then Camp Tallawanda's your only chance; trust me." TJ spoke with the arrogance that came from being a full head taller than almost everyone else his age, including Ricky.

"What do you do there?" Ricky began planning his talking points for his parents.

"Everything!"

"Like what?" He'd need details.

"Zip lining, hiking, swimming, fishing, there's girls. There's a blob. Lacrosse. Everything. And everybody goes."

"That does sound pretty neat—I mean cool," Ricky corrected himself.

"Are you going to be there?" TJ asked. "There's no shot you'll make any friends next year if you don't go."

"I don't know if my parent's would allow it," Ricky scratched his neck. "It sounds like too much fun. But I'll ask."

"If you don't go to Camp Tallawanda, you'll be the only kid in the whole town all summer. You'll show up to seventh grade literally not knowing a soul. Honestly, if you don't go, especially as the new kid, you'll be an automatic outcast—and no offense—but you'll probably a loser for the rest of your life. You gotta go."

"Okay. I'll ask," Ricky said without separating his teeth.

They made it all the way to the door of the school. Ricky wanted to go inside, but he could see TJ wasn't ready just yet. TJ turned back to the parking lot scanning for other friends.

"See that girl," TJ pointed across the lawn.

Ricky turned to see the prettiest girl he'd ever laid eyes on. She had long thick hair tied in a ponytail, long legs, and short shorts. In Ricky's old town, sixth grade girls never wore makeup. *She must be very mature for her age*, he thought.

"That's Hannah Havinghurst; she'll be at camp too."

"I'll ask 'em," Ricky nodded like a bobble head.

CHAPTER 2

Pulling Teeth

Mr. and Mrs. Collins, Dale and Marsha, were usually, if not always, strict. They never allowed Ricky to do anything. They didn't let him go on sleepovers, or have a dog, or watch cable TV. He couldn't dress-up as anything scary for Halloween. In fact, last Halloween he asked to be Count Dracula but his parents made him change it to the Count of Monte Cristo; nobody knew who he was. Convincing them he needed to go away for two months would be the toughest sell in his life.

They were bickering in the basement while unpacking boxes when he went for it. Mr. Collins already had a huge sweat stain showing through the back of his favorite navy blue college t-shirt. Mrs. Collins's pink long-sleeved shirt was dry, although she had on her old white sneakers she reserved for manual work, like gardening. Mrs. Collins contributed mostly by pointing and directing Ricky and Mr. Collins where things needed to go.

"So uh," Ricky swallowed to get some saliva into his dry mouth. He tried to talk over the pounding of his heart. "So, TJ from next door had a good suggestion for making friends."

"I'm not sure I'm a fan of those Stantons," his mom responded, instinctively laying the groundwork for a *No*.

"Did you guys do any research about the town before we moved?" Ricky massaged his entry.

"Marsha, what's in here, bricks?" Mr. Collins groaned trying to lift a box. He wiped his forehead and the long black hairs on his arms matted down from the sweat.

"Those are books, Dale."

"Look at this," Mr. Collins said to Ricky. "She brought all these books. Marsha why do we still have all of Ricky's toddler books? Who's reading these?"

"Just put them over there," she motioned to the back of the storage closet.

"This town has a really cool tradition," Ricky chimed in during the temporary silence.

"And what is that, dear?" Mrs. Collins put her hands on her knee giving Ricky her full attention.

"All the kids go to summer camp up in the mountains."

"Absolutely not," she said looking away from Ricky and back to make sure Mr. Collins put the books in the right spot. With the subtle turn of her head, she swiped the idea completely out of existence.

"Here's a good one; a book about baby teeth. Glad we packed this."

"Give it a rest, Dale."

"But everyone goes!" Ricky blurted.

He wondered if he picked the right time to bring this up. He had one chance, and already wanted to start over. There was no reasoning with these people. Everything was always just *No*.

"Son," Mr. Collins finally acknowledged this half of the conversation. "I doubt they *all* go. You talked to one kid. TJ doesn't know."

"Dad, that's all they were talking about at school. The whole day."

"We said no. Now hand me that box over here, that has all of our hangers."

"Then how am I going to make friends before starting junior high next year?"

"It's a big town, Richard. There's plenty of kids here," his mother explained.

"But you don't even know that! They'll be at Camp Tallawanda! I'm going to be the only kid starting seventh grade who doesn't go. All the other kids will be off having fun and I'll be home alone, like a loser."

"Richard, you aren't a loser," Mrs. Collins said, pivoting away from the main issue.

"That's what they said at school. Only losers don't go to summer camp."

"Maybe the losers are the only ones who *do* go to summer camp," Mr. Collins raised an eyebrow. "Did you ever think about it like that?"

"Dad, the teacher even told me I should go. And a lunch lady, and the hall monitors."

"Well what do they know?" Mrs. Collins asked. "Teachers don't know anything."

He'd have to pull out the big guns, "You promised when we moved you'd ease up on me and let me do stuff so I could make friends."

Then they really got into it.

He argued, he begged, and he reasoned that it wasn't fair that they forced an only child to move across the country with no friends. He warned his parents if he didn't go to summer camp, he'd probably turn out to be a loser with no friends. If he couldn't make friends, his parents would be breaking their promise they made when they told him about the move. Ricky pointed out he was getting older and it was time to let him have more freedom. Of course, his parents volleyed arguments back, always taking turns. They'd miss him too much. Having no friends didn't make him a loser. Two months was too long of a time to leave. He could make friends when all the kids came back from camp, etc. etc. etc.

Eventually, by some miracle—probably because they felt guilty for moving an only child across the country—but Ricky didn't care how, or why, but somehow, after what seemed like a marathon of arguing and logical reasoning, and phone calls made to other neighbors to verify that *all* the kids do in fact go, and yes it's safe, and no it's not too far, and the entire basement's worth of boxes, it ended. Ricky's parents agreed to Camp Tallawanda.

The next day, TJ came over to Ricky's new house and asked him for an update.

"They said I could go," Ricky beamed with two thumbs-up.

"Camp Tallawanda is going to change your life," TJ promised.

CHAPTER 3

Gearing Up

Ricky's butt barely hit the chair before his mother started grilling him that morning.

"Oh Richard, look at your hair!" she fussed. Mrs. Collins tried to pour some water in her hand and mat down Ricky's shaggy brown hair, but it stood straight up defying gravity.

They wouldn't eat another meal together for the whole summer, or at least until Parent's Weekend. Mrs. Collins cooked Ricky's favorite breakfast: sunny side up eggs with blueberry waffles and bacon. Mr. Collins had his laptop pulled up to the side of his chair as he often did in the mornings, usually to check the news. He logged onto Camp Tallawanda's website to review Ricky's camper profile.

"I'll tell ya son," Mr. Collins took a sip of his coffee, "I don't know how you convinced us to let you go away for six full weeks."

"And I don't like their cell phone policy," Mrs. Collins added. "I think they should let you have the cell phones."

"I actually think it's good to have the kids a little unplugged," Mr. Collins rebutted. "Lets them enjoy themselves, get some fresh air."

"How is he going to call us?"

"I'll call, Mom," Ricky promised.

"Everyday?" Mrs. Collins pretended to be asking a question but it was more of a command.

"As often as I can," Ricky didn't want to overcommit.

"I want you to make some other friends too," Mrs. Collins pointed with her fork. "I don't want you hanging around with that Stanton boy all summer. He has no manners whatsoever."

"And stay away from the girls," his dad advised. "You shouldn't have anything to do with girls at your age."

"You don't need to talk to a girl until you're married," Mrs. Collins explained.

Ricky put his hand on his forehead and slid it down his face. He took a quick peek at his watch. There'd be a couple more hours of lectures before getting dropped off at the bus.

"I won't talk to any girls," Ricky said, thinking about Hannah Havinghurst and her ponytail. "I'll follow all the rules, and I'll try not to have any fun."

"That's my boy," Mrs. Collins approved and took a sip of orange juice.

"We need to finish filling out Ricky's activity selections," Mr. Collins drew their attention to the laptop. "There seems to be a lot of character building activities."

"My boy doesn't need any character building. He could be teaching character building!"

"I already picked my classes," Ricky's chest started to tighten.

"Listen son," Mr. Collins said sternly. "You'll have plenty of time outside, but we pick your classes. That's a compromise. And that's that."

"Richard, honey," his mother took over to repeat most of what his father already said. "Your father and I love you very much. And we know this move was hard on you. But letting you go away for so long is hard on us too. While you're running around with all the other kids in town, we want to know you'll at least be learning something."

Ricky was almost too afraid to ask, "Like what?"

"Well for starters, instead of the Outdoor Adventure class, we decided to put you in Crafting Creatively."

Ricky's stomach dropped to his ankles, "But that's my favorite one!"

They responded to his outburst with closed-lipped stern faces and a long pause of silence. What choice did he have but to agree? He desperately wanted to go to camp. He wanted to hang out with TJ and make friends before junior high. Ricky would have to learn how to enjoy the crafting class. At least there'd be some girls in the class, he thought, trying to stay positive.

"Any others?" he almost whispered the question.

Then, the doorbell rang, and about three seconds later, it rang again.

"Well, that is just about the rudest thing I have ever heard," Mrs. Collins put her hand over her heart. "Who rings a doorbell like that?"

"It's wasting the batteries," Mr. Collins complained. "Ricky, go see who it is."

Then the doorbell rang again.

"Oh for Pete's sake!" Mrs. Collins slapped both hands on the table and got up to answer the door.

It was TJ Stanton.

"Good morning, Mrs. Collins," he said with a smile on his face.

"Hello, TJ. Are they going to be teaching you boys the proper etiquette for ringing doorbells at this camp?"

"Oh I sure hope so, Mrs. Collins. A growing boy like myself can never get enough etiquette."

"Never sounds about right," she said turning away to the kitchen. "Richard, Mr. Stanton is here to see you."

"And to what do we owe the pleasure so early this morning?" Mrs. Collins asked crossing her arms.

"Well ma'am, my parent's thought it would be beneficial for Ricky—as a first time camper and all—if I made sure he packed properly."

"Hey TJ," Ricky said running up to the front door, thankful for the lecture interruption.

"Grab your bag Rick, come over to my house, and we'll make sure you've got everything."

Ricky leaped over every other step on the way to his bedroom, leaving TJ alone with Mrs. Collins at the front door.

"Smells delicious in here, Mrs. Collins," TJ grinned.

When a person saw TJ Stanton's baby fat cheeks and perfectly parted to the side dark hair, if they didn't know any better, they'd think he was a well-behaved young man. Mrs. Collins knew better.

"It smells like something alright," she responded.

Ricky rumbled down the steps carrying his suitcase.

"I don't want you unpacking all that stuff Richard," she scolded as the two boys scrambled out of the house towards TJ's.

"I can't wait to see your lacrosse gear," TJ said.

"My what?"

"Your gear. What kind of gloves do you have? What stick do you shoot with?"

"Well actually," Ricky ran his hand over the front of his head down until he scratched the back of his neck. "I've never played lacrosse."

The confession screeched TJ to a full stop.

"What did you just say?"

"I've never played lacrosse before," Ricky spoke to the ground.

"So what do you play? Football? Basketball? Anything?"

"I can play piano," Ricky offered.

TJ put his hands on the back of his head and lifted his nose to the sky, "Come with me."

The two boys ran to TJ's garage. As the Stanton's garage door lifted from the ground, it revealed sports equipment, bicycles, roller blades, and all sorts of different toys.

"I'm spoiled," TJ said puffing his chest.

"I see that," Ricky nodded.

TJ pulled out a pair of padded gloves from a bin. They looked like hockey gloves. They were primarily white and black with powder blue stripes.

"You're going to need a set of gloves and a stick. The camp can supply you with everything else."

"These are neat," Ricky awed while putting on the gloves. They were thickly padded on the top and covered up his wrists, but the undersides were mesh and thin enough for him to wiggle his fingers and thumbs. They fit perfectly.

"Those are mine from last year. I get a new pair every year," TJ bragged. "You can have them for the summer."

Ricky admired the gloves on his outstretched hands, "No way? Thanks, man."

"Anyone showing up at camp without lacrosse gear is an automatic loser. I don't think anyone in this whole town doesn't have their own lacrosse gloves and stick, except you."

"Where I come from, we didn't play lacrosse. I don't even know what it is."

"It's the best sport in the world is what it is. Everyone here plays. If you want to have any friends in this town you'll need to be on the junior high lacrosse team."

TJ skateboarded to the other side of the garage. The wall was lined with hockey sticks, fishing poles, baseball bats, and something Ricky never saw before: lacrosse sticks. TJ pulled down two of them and gave one to Ricky.

"This is a lacrosse stick," TJ said holding up a three-foot long shiny aluminum pole. A white plastic, bell shaped head, with a string net in the middle rested at the top of the pole. The other end of the stick was taped up like a hockey stick or a baseball bat handle. Ricky felt the white plastic duckbill shaped top.

"That's the *head*," TJ explained. "The netting inside the head is called a *pocket*. The metal part is called the *shaft*. Together they make the *stick*."

"What are those long ones over there?" Ricky noticed some lacrosse sticks about as tall as him.

"Those are D-poles, for defensive players; I play defense. You won't play defense. Not big enough. If you're fast enough, you'll be playing midfield. *Middie* we call it," TJ pointed with his chin. "Take that short stick with you; keep it."

"No way? You're really giving it to me? Thanks man."

"Hey, I'm an only child too. If my next door neighbor doesn't have a stick and gloves, that means I'm playing catch alone."

Ricky grabbed his chrome lacrosse stick with his white, black, and powder blue gloves. He felt like some kind of superhero. He swung the stick like a baseball bat.

"How do you use this thing?"

"Geez, not like that. We'll get into the basics later. Oh, and I almost forgot, bring a cup."

"A cup?" Ricky scrunched his eyebrows. "What do you mean a cup?"

"This is a lacrosse ball," TJ handed Ricky a pale, smooth rubber ball. It was about the size of a baseball, a little heavier, and hard as a rock. "You don't want this ball hitting yours, you get it? A *cup*."

"Oh, a *cup*," Ricky blushed. "I thought you meant—you know—like a mug or something. Yeah. I have a cup."

"But I thought you didn't play sports?"

Ricky's parents bought him one, insisting he wore it during gym class, but he kept that information to himself. "I have one."

"Good. Cause you aren't borrowing one of mine," TJ laughed.

"Maybe though," Ricky paused staring out at his padded gloves and shiny new stick with a hand covering his mouth. "Maybe you can hold on to this stuff? And give them to me when we get there?"

"Parents?" TJ asked.

"I don't think my mom would like lacrosse," Ricky admitted. "Seems dangerous."

"You know, you're going to have to come out of the bubble at some point," TJ patted him on the back. "Don't worry, I'll cover for you."

TJ was the nicest, most helpful, but also the rudest kid Ricky had ever met.

CHAPTER 4

Welcome to Camp Tallawanda

Despite about two hundred or so campers waiting to get picked-up at Blue Creek West Elementary School, Ricky managed to find a perfect line of sight and locked in on Hannah Havinghurst. Her hot pink t-shirt matched her lipstick, and made Ricky's mouth water. His eyes followed her over to where she stood to meet the rest of her friends. As if she could feel his eyes on her, she turned her head over her shoulder and caught Ricky staring from the backseat of his parents' car window. He jerked his head away and could feel the hot rush of blood shooting into his embarrassed cheeks.

Well that's a good start.

The sun beamed through the cloudless sky, causing heat vibrations off the pavement while it fueled the energy of the students pouring in. The excitement of summer camp stirred the parking lot and everyone in it to a frenzy. Campers organized into groups based on the grades they'd be in after the summer, starting with those going into fourth grade. Ricky, TJ, and the other boys Ricky didn't get a chance to meet on his first and last day of school stood in the seventh grade section. Then Ricky noticed the kids that were all bigger and taller than everyone else. One of them in particular sported two collared polo shirts, pink and yellow, with both of the collars popped up.

"Who are those guys?" Ricky asked TJ. "I've never seen anyone wear two shirts like that."

"They'll be eighth graders next year at junior high," TJ shrugged only one shoulder. "Everybody gets picked up here cause it's easier for parents. Take a good look at those guys, and stay away from them. They're all a bunch of jerks, especially that one."

Ricky watched the boy in the pink and yellow shirts stomp on a soda can and then use his lacrosse stick to throw it across the lot. As the can flew through the air, it dripped on some younger kids standing under its path. They instinctively reached their hands to their wet necks raising their eyes to see what was the matter. The can landed smack in the middle of an open garbage container and the jerk high-fived one of his eighth grade buddies.

"Looks like it," Ricky agreed with TJ's assessment.

The camp rangers, with their clipboards, knee-high hiking socks, aviator sunglasses, and olive green drill sergeant hats, speed-walked the area checking off everyone's names, answering parents' questions, and directing students to their proper loading zones. The soon to be seventh grade boys shared the bus with next year's sixth grade boys. They loaded the girls on to their separate buses first. Ricky and TJ both watched as Hannah and her friends disappeared behind the bus doors.

Ricky's parents walked over to say goodbye to him one last time.

"Be good," they both said. "And make sure you call us."

"You don't have to sit next to TJ on the bus if you don't want to," his mother whispered. Ricky waved to his parents one last time as the buses turned out of the parking lot.

"How's it feel to step out of the bubble?" TJ patted Ricky's shoulder.

* * *

Camp Tallawanda was a few hours upstate from Ricky's new town. The buses had to navigate into the copper colored mountainside to get there. Ricky's old state hardly had any hills, so he could barely peel his eyes from out the window while they drove through the cliffs. Even from inside the bus, Ricky could smell the fresh pine scent from the tall ponderosa trees. Staring out the window helped him take his mind off the fact that this was about to be the longest he'd ever been away from home. Ricky's parents were the only two people he knew in the whole state, and now he'd be hours away from them all summer. He tried to focus back on the red stone mountains.

The boys watched movies to keep entertained, and for the most part, behaved. TJ introduced Ricky to some of the other seventh graders, but it seemed nobody cared much to talk to the new guy. They only wanted to share stories about old times at camp. Ricky had never been to camp before, so he had nothing to add to their conversation. He felt left out, and worried that maybe no one would talk to him the whole summer. He wondered if perhaps his parents were right, and maybe he shouldn't have come to camp at all.

The bus turned off down a gravel road through a pine tree forest. It was hard to believe there'd be anything but more trees and rocks down the hidden tight path, but suddenly, the buses stopped. Ricky could see the camp's entrance through the bus's front window. Wooden doors as a tall as a house, the kind used for an entrance of a castle, held up a sign as big as a scoreboard with orange painted letters that read: *CAMP TALLAWANDA.*

The boys went into a whirl of cheers, chants, and high-fives as the words on the sign split open for them to enter. Ricky joined in as everyone pounded the bus seats faster and harder while drowning out the creaking sound of the parting gates. The opened doors revealed a wide blue sky over a vast green valley. Log cabins sat on the far side of the grass field. The row of cabins and buildings stretched down a winding gravel trail for at least a half-mile. In the far back corner, a lake butted up against the tree line. All of Ricky's doubts about coming had vanished.

Standing in the front of the bus, a camp ranger howled through the speaker, "Welcome to Camp Tallawanda!"

The announcement caused another uproar from the boys. Ricky could hear the shouts and screams coming from the girls' buses too.

"Everybody off," the ranger shouted.

They rushed out like a mosh pit. Somebody elbowed Ricky right in the forehead, but his excitement kept him from hurting. The loose gravel kicked up dust, and made soft crunching sounds as the kids and buses pulled over into the unloading zone. Soon the whole entrance was inside a sandy cloud.

Each cabin along the trail had a little different personality than the one before it. Whether it was the windows, the colors of the doors, a stone slab chimney, or the shape of their porches, they each had a unique appearance. Ricky couldn't stop smiling.

"Dude, this is . . . " Ricky struggled for the right word.

"Neat?" TJ suggested and put his arm around Ricky's shoulder. "Drink it in pal, drink it all in," TJ took a long deep breath. After exhaling, he said, "Welcome to Camp Tallawanda."

CHAPTER 5

Salamander Cabin

"Okay! Seventh grade boys," the camp ranger at the bottom of the field cleared his throat into the megaphone. "If you're going into seventh grade next year, I need you over here." The boys from Ricky's bus sprinted to him.

"Who's our cabin leader?" Spencer Lutz, one of the kids Ricky met on the bus, asked. Spencer told a lot of jokes Ricky's mom wouldn't have wanted Ricky to hear. She would have been even more upset to see him laughing at them. Spencer was fascinated with human anatomy. Sometimes, Ricky wasn't sure whether he laughed at Spencer's jokes or at his long curly bleached hair sticking out of his baseball cap.

"I'm getting to that Mr. Lutz. My, we've all missed you up here," the camp ranger said as he adjusted his sunglasses.

"Well, hurry up; some of us got to pee," Spencer said looking around for laughs. He got an encouraging amount.

"Your cabin leader is Heath McPhair," the camp ranger explained. He pointed over to an iron cattle fence along the dirt trail where most of the cabin leaders sat. The whole cabin took off sprinting as soon as Heath raised his hand.

Of all the college-aged kids who worked as cabin leaders, Heath was easily the coolest option. He had clean-cut hair, broad shoulders, he wore his camp shirt untucked from his khaki shorts, and he tied his sneakers loose in a knot underneath the tongue, so as not to show the end of his laces. He came off as the type of guy in a movie who would tease the superhero in high school before the superhero got his powers. But, if Heath worked as a cabin leader at a summer camp, he must be nicer than that, Ricky hoped.

"What's up, guys? Welcome to Camp Tallawanda. I'm Heath McPhair; I'm your cabin leader. Is everyone here?"

Heath pulled out a wrinkled piece of paper from his pocket.

"Okay, if you're here, raise your hand. I'm going to run through this list one time fast. If you don't hear your name tell me at the end. Ready?"

The campers nodded. After Heath read through the names, he counted and confirmed the number of kids in front of him matched his paper. In total, there were twenty boys in Ricky's cabin for the summer.

Then Heath continued, "I've spent plenty of summers at Camp Tallawanda as a camper and as a cabin leader. I even did one summer in high school as a staffer. I know all the ins and outs, and all the unwritten rules, and all about the dos and don'ts. I don't want any problems, and I don't want to have to be a problem." Heath rubbed his hands together. "I came here to have fun too. I'll stay out of your hair so long as you all do what I say. Are we clear?"

"Clear!" They nodded.

"This is going to be the best summer ever," TJ whispered to Ricky and Spencer.

"What cabin we got?" the tallest and strongest boy in the group asked. He even made TJ look short.

"Whoa big fella, are you sure you're supposed to be going into seventh grade?" Heath asked pulling out the attendance sheet again. "Not high school? What's your name?"

"Dane Zamborowski," the tall shaggy-haired giant answered.

"Dane Zam-what?" Heath squinted. "You play lacrosse? Defense I'm guessing."

"Duh," Dane shrugged.

"Well, how about we just call you Great Dane?" Heath made a note on his paper while Great Dane smiled in approval of his new nickname.

Some of the other boys chimed in asking which cabin they'd been assigned. When Heath announced they were in *Salamander* cabin, the boys bolted in the same direction. Ricky would find out later that Salamander cabin was the one closet to the lake. It was considered one of, if not *the* best cabin at camp. Ricky picked up his bag and chased the group. He cruised his way up to the front of the pack, but he didn't know where he was going and had to slow down to follow someone.

"Who dat kid?" Dane asked TJ after Ricky whizzed past them. "He the new guy?"

"That's Ricky," TJ explained.

"He a middie," Great Dane decided.

Salamander was a genuine old-fashioned log cabin, built from solid pine trees. Its base and steps were made of cobblestones. Salamander had a forest green painted roof with matching window shutters. A blond wood porch stocked with red beach chairs and a swinging bench circled the front of the cabin. The others raced inside, but before he entered, Ricky paused to read the overhead sign: *Salamander, est. 1906.*

The cabin had two main rooms: The first room housed the bunk beds, and each bunk bed had a large two-drawer trunk to be shared by the bunkmates. The second room was a game room; the campers called it the Den. The Den included a pool table, a foosball table, checkers, cards, and some open area for seating. There was even a crowded bookshelf, but no television or computers. The cabin also had a large bathroom with private showers. The seventh graders took turns shouting to each other the next amazing feature they found.

On the bus ride, TJ and the others discussed the importance of choosing a good bunk and a good bunkmate. They argued about whether the top or bottom bunk was preferable. Being stuck on the inside seat, boxed in by TJ and his loud mouth, Ricky didn't have much opportunity to share his opinion, but he preferred the top-bunk. He almost spoke out to explain his reasoning, but decided against it, fearing he might persuade the other campers. Mrs. Collins convinced her son he wouldn't like the thought of dirty campers sitting on his bed sheets all summer. Also, not that it would be likely to happen, but if the bed broke, he'd rather be on the top. But Ricky kept quiet about all that, and luckily for him, most of the seventh graders preferred the bottom bunk.

According to the guys, not only was it important to get a good bunk, and a good bunkmate; it was equally important to get good bunk neighbors. When TJ, Spencer, and Great Dane ran over to a corner to claim their beds, Ricky followed.

"Big guy's spot right here," Great Dane threw his canvas duffle bag on the bottom bunk.

Another boy, almost as big as Dane, dropped his bag on the top bed. Dane and the other defender were easily the largest in the cabin. TJ was the same height as them, but a little thinner. TJ put his brand new black sports bag on the bunk next to Dane's. Ricky tried to put his suitcase on the bed above TJ's, but the funny kid with the curly blonde hair threw his bag on the bed too.

"What do you think you're doing?" Spencer Lutz asked Ricky.

"I wanted to bunk with TJ," Ricky answered looking to TJ for support.

"You don't play defense, do you?" Spencer asked while tossing Ricky's bag back to him.

"Ricky, you got to share a bunk with guys who play the same position as you," TJ explained.

Ricky didn't understand.

"In lacrosse," TJ grunted. "Me and these big goons play defense. Spencer is the goalie; that's defense too, so he goes with us."

"What am I?" Ricky asked.

"Middie," Great Dane and TJ said at the same time.

Ricky hid his hurt feelings by forcing a smile. He picked the top bunk on the other side of TJ and Spencer's, but nobody claimed the spot under him.

"Goin' solo, huh?" Ricky's neighbor asked. The boy was the same height as Ricky, but much pudgier with short black hair and wearing an orange football jersey.

"Name's Artie Gonzales, I play attack."

"You ride the bench," Spencer corrected Artie.

"What's attack?" Ricky asked.

"I'll tell ya what, new guy," Artie pointed. "Do yourself a favor: go in the library and read *How to Play Lacrosse*."

"Why don't you read it first, Art?" Spencer butt in again.

"Hey man, don't listin' to these clowns," a southern accent said putting his bag on the bottom of Ricky's bunk. His long hair, much longer than Ricky's parents would ever allow, was slicked back away from his face. "I'm Mason Ellis, 'cept ever-body calls me Ace." He stuck his hand out, and Ricky shook it. "I was the new kid last year, comin' from Laredo, Texas. I play middie too. Stick with me, partner. I'll show you 'round."

Thanks to Ace, Ricky was introduced to the rest of the guys. Everybody knew Ace, and it seemed they all liked him. He walked around giving high-fives or secret handshakes to just about the whole cabin. Ricky was relieved he wouldn't need to count on TJ to be the only one sticking up for him all summer. He thought he'd actually be able to make some friends before junior high started after all.

CHAPTER 6

Falcon Cabin

After being shown their cabins, and claiming their bunks, they had to report to the Grand Hall for a camp-wide dinner. The Grand Hall was the largest building on the campgrounds. Its exterior was made from redwood tree logs. Stone slab steps lead up to the massive double-door entrance. Its wooden doors had ram's horns for handles.

The ceiling in the Grand Hall rose high and exposed the wooden beams that supported the roof. Deer antler chandeliers hung down from black iron chains. The dinner tables in the Grand Hall were designed to be long enough to hold about as many campers as fit inside of a cabin, and there were enough tables to fit the entire camp. All of the twenty boys from Salamander cabin shuffled in seeking their assigned table. Ricky sat next to TJ; luckily nobody made him move his seat because of some other unwritten rule he didn't know.

"Oh wow, we get waiters?" Ricky observed.

"That's right, young man," one of the camp rangers said as he walked by the boys' table. "Everything at Camp Tallawanda is designed to give our campers the best possible experience imaginable. Most of these servers are high school students now, and former Camp Tallawanda campers. Maybe you'll come back some day and be a server, or a cabin leader?"

"Look who's sitting next to us," Artie in the football jersey said leaning over the table. "It's the seventh grade girls. Jackpot."

Ricky eyed down the table. Hannah and her other cabin mates approached directly towards the Salamander boys. Ricky noticed the nametag on their table was *Falcon*. He asked if they knew where that cabin was.

"Well that's just great," Artie complained. "Falcon's the farthest cabin from ours."

"They don't map these places out on accident, guys," Heath said while spotting the Falcon cabin leader, an attractive college-aged girl about his age.

All the boys, and even Heath, went silent and stared as Hannah and her cabin took their seats at the table right next to them. Ricky kept his focus on Hannah, but Heath and the rest of the Salamanders took in every detail of the dark-haired, green-eyed, tanned and toned Falcon cabin leader.

"Hey there Falcons," Heath said standing up with his hand outstretched. "I'm Heath McPhair, Salamander cabin leader."

"Geez, he doesn't waste any time," Spencer joked to TJ.

"I'm Brittney Cannon," she smiled. She shook Heath's hand. "Hey there Salamanders," Brittney waived to the table, knowing full well the effect a twenty-year-old girl has on twelve-year-old boys. They responded by looking straight to the floor or into the ceiling. The Falcon girls would have rolled their eyes if they saw the way the Salamander boys looked at Brittney, but they were too busy ogling Heath.

"Well, we'll have to make sure we don't plan any events at the same time, Brittney. We should keep this crowd separated all summer," Heath grinned.

"Yes, we don't want to have to worry about you boys playing any pranks on our cabin either," Brittney warned, and the Salamander boys chuckled.

"What does she mean about pranks?" Ricky asked Ace.

"Oh they'll be plenty o' pranks 'round here," Ace responded.

"I'm going to pretend I didn't hear that," Heath smirked at Ace.

TJ leaned over to Ricky and said, "All the cabins play pranks on everybody else."

"It's tradition," Ace added. "Las' year, we took all them fifth grade boys' pillows an' threw 'em on the roof of their cabin. Stuff like that."

"Will people prank us?" Ricky worried.

"Not if they too scared a what you gonna do back to them," Great Dane shook his head.

"All the cabin leaders know about it too," TJ went on. "But if you're smart about it, they won't get you in trouble."

"All right dudes, that's enough of all that for now," Heath said from across the table. "Here comes dinner."

Ricky never tasted better food. They served southwestern barbeque beef brisket, with sides of the thickest, and creamiest macaroni and cheese he ever had. The waiters brought everything right to the table. If anyone wanted seconds, or a refill or a new fork, the waiters came running over to tend to every request.

"Is there anything that isn't awesome here?" Ricky asked TJ.

"No TV," Great Dane answered.

"No TV?" Ricky asked pretending to be upset. He didn't care about TV; his parents hardly ever let him watch TV, especially during the summer.

"What do you need a TV for?" Heath asked from across the table, establishing to the campers he could hear everything. "From what they tell me Rick, you should be spending most of your time playing wall ball."

The whole table laughed. Ricky knew he had been insulted, but he didn't understand why. The blank look on his face, and the fact his cheeks weren't even turning red, let everyone else know Ricky didn't get the joke.

"You need practice," Dane explained.

"What is wall ball?" Ricky asked.

"It's exactly what it sounds like," Spencer said, grabbing two more helpings of corn bread off of the passing waiter's tray. "You go outside and find a brick wall, and you play catch with the wall."

"Don't worry, Rick," Heath reassured him. "We'll help you learn. You want to make the junior high team next year don't you?"

"I hadn't thought about it," Ricky confessed.

"If you don't make the lacrosse team next year, you can forget about talking to girls for the rest of your life," TJ warned.

Ricky glanced over at Hannah, then Brittney, then the rest of the girls' table, and asked, "Where's the closest brick wall?"

"Look at this dude," TJ chuckled. "Ricky Collins's been here for an hour and already coming out of his bubble."

CHAPTER 7

Porcupine Cabin

"Is this safe?" Ricky asked.

The first morning, the Salamander boys listened to Heath's advice, and wore their swim trunks to breakfast. After eating, they ditched their shirts and ran out to be the first ones at the zip line. To get there, they had to hike up the back of the camp's main trail. The zip line tower sat on top of the camp's tallest hill; technically it was a small mountain. They could see for miles in all directions at the top of the tower. Ricky, Ace, and TJ lined up to be the first zip line riders of the summer. TJ insisted on going first.

"Is this safe?" He asked again.

"Not really," TJ hooked himself onto the cable wire that stretched for what seemed like a mile down to the lake. He curled his toes around the edge of the launch point. Nothing separated him from the tops of the trees and the ground a long way down below. "But it's the fastest way to get back to the lake."

The staff lifeguard checked TJ's harness rather carelessly and gave him a thumbs-up. Without hesitating, TJ shouted '*Cowabunga!*' and jumped off the platform. He whipped his way down the long path until a minute later spinning and splashing at the end of the line into the lake.

"Alright, you're up dude," the lifeguard said to Ricky.

"Aren't there any instructions?" Ricky asked.

"You're at Camp Tallawanda, man," the lifeguard chuckled. "Have fun."

Ricky stood at the edge of the platform. After seeing how easily TJ jumped off without any fear, he didn't want to show fear in front of Ace and the other Salamander guys watching.

"See ya at the blob!" Ricky gasped to Ace. He took a deep breath and jumped off the platform.

The wind rushed over his face as the zip line picked up speed. He felt like he was flying. The wheels on the zip line hissed as they rotated around the metal cable. He soared directly over some of the cabin buildings, through the tree line, and eventually over the lake. Spotting the tops of campers' heads far below him, he felt like a soaring hawk. Ricky let out a long howl as he glided over a group of campers walking up the trail on their way to the zip line platform. As the water got closer, he tried to lift himself up for as long as possible until he came splattering down into the lake. The water was colder than expected, and he felt the goose bumps raise all over his body with a jolt from the cold. His adrenaline rush kept him warm.

"That is so neat!" Ricky yelled to TJ who waited for him on the dock. "Help me unhook myself."

"Dude, you're helpless," TJ said jumping back into the lake. "Let's hit the blob next."

They couldn't get there fast enough. The blob was a giant floating yellow, red, and blue stripped bag of air, about the size of a school bus. Ricky had never seen one before, but the concept seemed simple. One camper sat at the front end of the blob, and another camper jumped off the 15-foot platform on the back end. Then, when the jumper landed, all the air moved to the front, launching whoever sat there way up into the air, and eventually, into the water.

"You go first this time," TJ suggested when they got to the top of the platform.

"Why?"

"Because, I'm heavier than you, I'll launch you higher than you can launch me," TJ explained.

A young fourth grade boy, who probably weighted only seventy-five pounds, and barely fit inside of his lifejacket, sat on the front of the blob waiting for Ricky to jump.

"What's taking so long?" the little boy yelled kicking his feet with anticipation.

"Don't bite your tongue," the lifeguard instructed the boy.

Ricky leapt as high as he could and came smashing down on the blob. To the delight of everyone watching, the young camper belly-flopped into the water. The campers in line applauded for the splash and sound of the smack of his body against the lake.

"Okay Ricky, are you ready down there?" TJ asked after Ricky crawled his way over to the far end of the plastic float.

"I think so," Ricky chattered his teeth. He couldn't see when TJ was going to jump. The anticipation felt like a blender in his stomach.

"Don't bite your tongue," the lifeguard shouted again.

"Okay, on the count of three, Rick," TJ called out form the platform. "One ..."

Wham!

Ricky went soaring as high as the platform. His arms flailed and his feet kicked frantically as he screamed. He should have suspected TJ wouldn't count all the way to three. The force of the launch caused him to turn upside down, and he landed head first into the lake. When he made his way to the surface, the campers gave him a shouting ovation. The better the splash, the better reaction from the crowd of kids waiting their turn.

"How was it?" TJ shouted over to Ricky.

"You freakin' jerk!" Ricky slapped his hand against the water. "I'm getting back in line!"

* * *

The first day went by in a flash. Ricky had a smile on his face the whole time. In the first week of camp, the boys spent their mornings trading off between the blob and the zip line. In the afternoons, they usually went to the pool, or to the go-karts course, or both. After dinner, they had an on-going pool and Ping-Pong tournament in the Den of their cabin.

On one of the last mornings before the class sessions started, the Salamander boys planned on going straight to the zip line after breakfast. But when they walked out of the dining hall, the eighth graders from the Porcupine cabin were waiting to confront them. The group of older boys stood at the base of the Grand Hall's steps. Every one of them had their lacrosse sticks and wore the same blue and white junior high issued lacrosse jersey.

"Hey losers," one of the bigger kids said from the middle of the group. "Are you dorks going to run around in the kiddie pool again all day, or do you want to play some lax?"

No one from Salamander said anything. They froze at the top of the steps with nowhere to go.

"Yeah, I'd be scared too if I was you," another one of them said. He wore the number one jersey, and his gloves were solid blue. Ricky recognized him as the kid from the parking lot wearing the pink and yellow collared shirts.

"We're not scared!" TJ shouted back at him.

"Well you should be," said number one. "Cause I'm going to make sure you're picking grass out of your facemask all morning."

The eighth graders laughed at number one's threat.

"You have fifteen minutes to be at Cooke Field. If you don't show up, you can count on getting a visit from us tonight," number one warned.

After they walked away, and no longer in hearing distance, Spencer called after them, "Yeah? Well, I'll block your crappy shots all day!"

"Good one, Spencer," TJ rolled his eyes.

"Who was that guy?" Ricky asked. "The guy in the number one jersey?"

"Zach Taylor, biggest freakin' jerk in town," Ace answered.

"Last year, those guys pranked us practically twice a week," added Artie. "Remember when they stole all our socks?"

"Is that allowed?" Ricky asked sounding more concerned than he wanted to give away.

"Come on guys," TJ encouraged them. "Are we just gonna stand around or are we going to play those guys?"

"We ain't even practiced," said Great Dane.

"It doesn't matter! We have to play them," TJ argued.

"If we don't show up," Artie started to say with his head down. "Then those guys are gonna torture us all summer. We gotta play."

"Art, you're not even a starter."

"Shut up, Spencer. So what?" Artie shot back, "At least I'm not scared."

"I'll do it," Ace chimed in to break up the argument.

"Yeah, same," said Great Dane.

The rest of the cabin agreed. Nobody wanted to know what the consequences would be for backing down from the eighth graders so early in the summer. They had to accept the challenge.

Back at the Salamander cabin, they scrambled to put on their lacrosse gear. Ricky stood around not really sure what he should be doing. Great Dane had on his cleats, pads, and a black and green lacrosse jersey as he shouted around orders to encourage everyone to get dressed faster.

Because he played goalie, Spencer, wore different shoulder pads than the rest of the guys. His stick also had a much bigger head than everyone else's. It reminded Ricky of a pool cleaning tool. Spencer finally managed to get his head through his red and yellow jersey when he saw Ricky standing there doing nothing.

"What are you looking at?" Spencer asked Ricky.

"I don't have any pads," Ricky answered.

"Then go get some!" Spencer shouted at him pointing to the Den.

"Ricky, come on with me," Ace offered. "That back closet's got a bunch o' gear. There's elbow pads an' everythin'."

Helmets, elbow pads, shoulder pads, gloves, and even some sticks and cleats that Camp Tallawanda collected over the years filled the closet. The camp bought some of the gear new; the rest was donated, or forgotten and never claimed. Ricky had TJ's borrowed gloves and stick, but needed everything else. They fumbled through the bin to find a pair of grey and red elbow pads that covered up his biceps and went halfway down his forearms.

"Here, put these on," Ace tossed him a pair of black shoulder pads.

Ricky needed help putting them on. Lacrosse shoulder pads seemed flimsy, but they did allow for him to move his arms around comfortably.

"Hope you got your own cup," Ace said.

"I do."

Before Ricky could hardly get the words out of his mouth, Ace gave him a gentle whack with his lacrosse stick to make sure Ricky was indeed wearing his cup.

"Hey!"

"Just checkin'," Ace laughed.

"Oh, I want this jersey," Ricky grabbed into the box to pull out a red jersey with a green dinosaur and a purple number 45 on it. The reverse white side had the same green dinosaur with the number 45 written in red. Finally, he grabbed a helmet. A bin offered all sorts of sizes and different color helmets, but the one that fit him best was plain white, with a shiny chrome facemask.

"How the heck can you guys see with these things?" Ricky asked with his helmet on. He never wore a helmet with a facemask before. He kept going cross-eyed trying to see out through the chrome bars.

Ace laughed at him, "You'll get used to it, after awhile."

He tossed a ball towards Ricky, he swatted at it, but it bonked off his facemask. Ace, TJ, and Spencer all laughed.

"Lesson one," Ace explained. "The ball don't got any teeth, it ain't gonna hurtchya."

"I can't see anything," Ricky said starting to take off his helmet.

"Then leave your helmet on and get used to it," commanded Spencer. "The sooner the better. Come on guys, let's go!"

The Salamander cabin ran in an unorganized mass of mismatched lacrosse jerseys and equipment, when suddenly everything went into slow motion. The seventh grade girls from Falcon walked across the street just ahead of them. They were headed for the pool. Every last one of them strutted across the trail in their bathing suits and sunglasses.

Although they were late for a showdown, all of the Salamander crew slowed their pace to gaze with wide-eyes at the girls in bathing suits. Hannah and her friend Kristin lead the pack, carrying their towels down at their sides. They had matching turquois bikinis, low cut with little ruffles on the bottoms. Neither Hannah nor her brown haired friend managed to do so much as tilt their heads in the direction of Ricky, or any of the other guys.

"Won't even look at us," Artie observed.

"Those two only want to talk to eighth graders," TJ confirmed.

"Great Dane, you're getting the green light from that one," one of the guys noticed. Great Dane spotted the tall dark haired girl in the back. She stared at Dane without blinking, and he stared right back at her.

"Key is don't look away first," Dane explained.

Hannah and Kristin continued to refuse to look at Ricky. As he scanned the rest of the troop, he saw a blonde curly haired girl in the middle. Their eyes locked for a quick second, then they darted their eyes away and stumbled. After the boys crossed the Falcon cabin's path, they could smell the cloud of perfume left in the girl's wake. Once the flower scented mist cleared, the Salamanders resumed focus on the task at hand. It was game time.

CHAPTER 8

Showdown at Cooke Field

"They're going to clobber us," Artie said as they got to the field.

When they saw the Salamanders approached they banded to together at the edge of the field. The eighth graders stood shoulder-to-shoulder, arms crossed and helmets on ready to go. Compared to the seventh graders' hodgepodge collection of mismatched jerseys and equipment, the Porcupine cabin's matching royal blue and white uniforms made the towering older kids appear much more impressive.

"You losers have to turn your jerseys to the white side," Zach Taylor, number one, shouted. "We all match in blue."

"TJ? Where should I go?" Ricky asked.

"On the sidelines to watch." Spencer answered for TJ. "Have you ever even seen anyone play lacrosse before?"

"No." Ricky admitted, grateful he wouldn't have to play. He still couldn't see through his facemask.

Two camp staffers sat in a lifeguard-like tower on the middle edge of Cooke Field. Their lawn chairs sat face to face so they could talk to each other but also keep an eye on everything. They had their shirts off with sunglasses on. When the boys took the field in their lacrosse gear, one of them blew his whistle and spoke into his megaphone:

"What are you guys doing in full pads?"

"We're having a nice friendly scrimmage," Zach Taylor explained.

Ricky assumed the camp staffers would force them to call off the game, or least not let them play in full pads. The staffers talked amongst themselves for about a minute. One of them spoke into his walkie-talkie but Ricky couldn't hear what he said. They consulted a supervisor to determine whether they'd need more adults around. The scratch from the walkie-talkie answered back, but again Ricky couldn't make out the words.

"Okay," the staffer said and gave them a thumbs-up. "Be careful."

Both cabins cheered. Game on. The starters took their faceoff positions.

Zach turned to his goalie behind him and shouted, "Nolan, you ready?"

"Doesn't matter!" Nolan, the fat eighth grade goalie yelled back. He clanked the back of his stick against both of the goal posts. "These scrubs aren't bringing the ball down here."

Zach placed the ball at the centerline. He and Ace both crouched down to it, with the heads of their lacrosse sticks parallel outside the ball. When one of the eighth graders on the sideline yelled "Go," Ace and Zach tried to clamp their sticks down over the ball. Zach clinched his stick first, and in a sweeping motion pushed the ball over to his teammate. The Porcupine midfielder scooped it quickly in stride. The game officially started.

The best players could pass right on a line into the head of a stick. Once a guy had the ball, he constantly twisted his wrists to keep it from falling out of the pocket. Everybody swatted at his gloves and arms, doing anything to knock the ball loose. When the ball hit the ground, guys got full on body-checked trying to pick it up. Metal lacrosse shafts and plastic heads clanking into each other echoed throughout the field. Ricky had never seen anything like this.

"Is it always this rough?" Ricky asked Artie.

Artie had the hairiest legs Ricky had ever seen. But he could stick handle as good as anyone. He constantly showed off his skills, treating his stick like a baton. But as Spencer often reminded him, ball handling wasn't catching and throwing, which was why Artie stood on the sideline next to Ricky.

"Yeah it's a violent sport," Artie shrugged. "We don't have refs out here though. Some of this isn't allowed; can't push in the back and stuff like that."

"What about the whacking with the sticks?"

"That's pretty much okay," Artie patted his arm pads. "That's what these are for."

Zach and his teammates managed to work the ball down towards the seventh grade goal area, the *box*. They passed the ball back and fourth flawlessly. While the eighth graders displayed their passing skills on offense, on the other end of the field, the three seventh grade attacks, and the three eighth grade defenders stood at the centerline, but didn't cross it.

"Why aren't those guys doing anything down there?" Ricky asked.

Artie shook his head; "Each team can only have seven players on the defensive side of the field: three middies, three defenders and a goalie. But you only get six players on the scoring side of the field. So our three attacks and their three defenders wait for the ball to cross the line."

Ricky counted the guys on the field, "So, the three middies can go on both sides?"

"There ya go!" Artie smiled. "You're learning."

Then, bang!

Zach Taylor launched a shot, whizzing it over Spencer's shoulder and into the net.

"That guy's pretty good," Artie admitted to Ricky.

"Hey goalie! That's what I call my signature Taylor Phaser," Zach said while making a motion as if shooting a bow and arrow.

"And a show-off," Artie added.

"A phaser wouldn't be a bow and arrow, it's actually—" Ricky started to explain.

"—Dude," Artie interrupted. "No one cares."

While the teams walked back to midfield for another faceoff, Ace came jogging towards the sidelines tapping the top of his helmet, signaling he needed a sub.

Ace rested both hands on his knees and wheezed, "These guys are clobberin' us like dusty rugs out there."

"Lacrosse is pretty neat," Ricky said to Ace. "Wish I could play."

"And there's another Taylor Phaser for the scoreboard!" Zach exclaimed, putting his stick in an imaginary sword sheathe. He had already won the faceoff and scored another goal.

"Mark my words, man," Ace huffed. "We're gonna play these goons again, and it won't be no scrimmage next time. It'll be a real game. So you better learn quick," he gave a thud to Ricky's shoulder pads to make sure his words sunk in. "Cause we need some help."

Zach Taylor went out for a rest, and Ace went back in. Finally, the seventh graders got the ball to their offensive side, where Marcus Jones waited at attack. Marcus Jones was the best on the team. He wore yellow gloves and had the body structure of an Olympic sprinter. He took the pass from Ace and dodged his defender. He swung his stick like a golf club and scored. The seventh graders huddled around him cheering.

But the celebration didn't last. Zach came out onto the field. He won the next faceoff over Ace, and the Porcupines went right back to work on offense.

"What do you think that defender is saying down there to Dez?" Ricky motioned to the guys standing at midfield.

"Nothing nice," Artie ensured him.

Desmond 'Dez' Miller prided himself on his perfectly cylindrical flattop hairstyle; he said it made him look taller. However, with his flattop matted down under his sweaty lacrosse helmet, Dez couldn't hide his small size. He barely stood eye-level with the defender's collarbone. Despite his stature, he was considered the best scorer after Marcus and Ace.

"Are you Desmond Miller?" the big long pole asked him.

Dez didn't answer.

"Janet Miller's your older sister, right? She's two years older?"

"How do you know?" Dez took a side step away from the unfriendly giant.

The defender took a step closer to Dez, "I made out with her last year."

"She still has the dog breath," Dez answered.

The eighth grader stepped on the back of Dez's heel and crosschecked him from behind, knocking him to the ground.

"Hey! What's your problem!" Dez blurted. Then he fearlessly swung his stick at the defender's shins. The big defender jumped on top of Dez. Marcus and the other seventh grade attack heard the commotion and sprinted over, with their defenders chasing right behind them. Nolan ran out of the eighth grade goal to join in on the ruckus.

"Fight! Fight!" several boys from the benches yelled.

The two camp staffers who had long since stopped paying attention to the game popped up from their seats and radioed in to the Camp Rangers for assistance.

Both sides went flying to the center of the field where Dez and the defender wrestled to the ground. Mayhem ensued. They pushed, punched, and pulled down each other's jerseys. Ricky had never been in a fight, but thought it would be exciting. He ran towards the heart of the mess, unsure of what to do once he got there. He instantly got knocked in the face. Luckily, with his helmet on, it didn't really hurt. Then, someone whacked him in the stomach, which brought him to his knees. The pile toppled over him, and soon the knot of people trampled over Ricky and anyone else on the ground.

A camp ranger sprinted to the center of Cooke Field so quickly that his hat fell off and dangled from the string around his neck. The booming sound of his air horn broke up the scuffle.

"Stop it! Stop it! Stop it!" the ranger shouted pulling guys off of the ground.

Dez had a black eye, so did the eighth grader who started the fight. It seemed everyone had signs of the quarrel, except Zach Taylor. Zach didn't have a scratch on him, which meant he must have sat back and watched the whole thing. *What a worm*, Ricky thought as the camp ranger and two staffers continued to separate the teams.

"What is going on out here?" the ranger bellowed. He had put his drill sergeant hat back on, and adjusted his knee socks and sunglasses. "Somebody better speak up." His deep voice echoed as loud as a fire truck.

He glared with a clenched jaw behind his mustache at the two staffers who should have been supervising. "Well what happened?" he demanded.

Both the two shirtless staffers stood with one arm down and the other holding an elbow. They shifted the weight on their feet. The first staffer cleared his throat and whispered, "Well sir, obviously, we were monitoring the game with our undivided attention, obviously." He coughed again, "And while the ball was down on this side of the field sir, that's where we were watching. Obviously, for safety purposes. But then a fight broke out on the other end. It happened so fast; I couldn't be sure who started it. Sir."

"I concur," the second staffer nodded. "Sir."

"You two get back to your post. I'll handle this," the ranger grunted.

The campers from both sides avoided eye contact with the camp ranger's sunglasses by looking at the ground. Ricky felt his heart about to beat out of his chest. He glanced over to TJ, who signaled for Ricky to keep quiet with the slightest shake of his head.

"Mr. Desmond Miller?" the camp ranger whirled around, Ricky would find out eventually this was Ranger Howard. "Would you care to explain as to why it is that you have a black-eye?"

"I'm sorry, sir," Dez beamed at the eighth grade defenseman who gave it to him. "I can't remember."

"And what about you, Mr. Patrick Winkerton?" Ranger Howard asked the boy who started the whole thing. "What do you have to say about all this?"

Patrick Winkerton stood stone-faced.

Ranger Howard squared himself to Patrick. He stepped forward, standing only inches away. He leaned his head in further so the brim of his hat stopped bent against Patrick's sweaty forehead, just below Patrick's brown curly hairline.

"Are you going to tell me how you got that bloody nose, Mr. Winkerton?"

Staring eye to eye with his own pale reflection through the ranger's sunglasses, Patrick started to cry.

"I don't know," Patrick lied, wiping the tears from his eyes.

"Call Patty's *mommy*," a voice from the group teased, followed by the laughter of all the seventh graders. The camp ranger jumped-doing a 180 spin in the air-and pulled his sunglasses off.

"Who said that?" Ranger Howard growled. "Gosh dang it! I said who said that?"

Ricky's knees shook from fear, but guys like Ace and TJ had to bite their lips to keep from laughing at the joke.

"That's it! Nobody wants to tell me what happened? You're cracking jokes! I revoke all seventh and eighth grade boys' blob privileges until further notice."

Groans and pleas for mercy came from both sides.

"You've all had your chance. Now all of you go on and get out of here."

Walking back to the cabin, the Salamanders cursed at Spencer Lutz. There was no denying the squirrely sarcastic voice that blurted out the 'mommy' comment belonged to him. Spencer tried to explain their blob privileges would have been taken away whether he said it or not. Not everyone agreed with Spencer. But they all agreed they needed to practice. There was no way they'd make it all summer without another showdown with the jerks from Porcupine cabin. Nobody said it, but they all thought it: *Those guys are good.*

CHAPTER 9

Lacrosse 101

It wasn't until the daylight of the next morning before the boys of Salamander cabin figured out how the attack happened. But that night, after they fought the eighth graders, the guys from Porcupine cabin conducted Camp Tallawanda's first prank of the summer. In the dark of night, while the Salamander cabin was sound asleep, the eighth graders snuck up to their front door, and surrounded the cabin on all sides. Patrick Winkerton, and the goalie Nolan Stier, went to the front door laying out a long plastic tarp full of mud, soap, and cracked eggs. Zach Taylor and one of the other goons carried another tarp around to the back door.

The eighth graders put the last of the cracked eggs, and mud on both of the tarps, and then covered them heavily in soap to make sure they were as slick as possible. After they set the tarps in place, they threw smoke bombs and shouted into the windows, "Fire! Fire! Wake up! Wake up! It's a fire!"

They boys bolted into the woods, so they'd be far enough not to be seen, but close enough to hear what happened next.

The terrified seventh graders sprang awake. They jumped out of their beds. The boys in the top bunks came crashing down on anyone who might have been running by underneath them. In their tired haze, the confused seventh graders believed there was a real fire, much to the delight of the eighth graders listening and laughing in the woods. They came barreling out of the cabin from both ends at top speed, all of them barefoot and in their pajamas or underwear. In a mass of chaos, they slid and tumbled over each other on the wet dirty tarps. When TJ ran out of the cabin onto the tarp, his feet went flying straight out from under him, and he landed painfully on his butt down the steps. Great Dane had the same experience when he ran out of the back door.

Everyone except Heath McPhair lay on the ground and suffering from fear, confusion, or minor injuries. Heath had been a camper and cabin leader for long enough to recognize a prank. But in the confusion, he couldn't do much to calm his cabin before they darted for the doors.

Technically, Camp Tallawanda rules forbid any camper to vandalize, intrude, tamper, disrupt, or in any other way interfere with another camper's quiet enjoyment of the campgrounds. This rule was loop-holed by the clause that stated a Camp Tallawanda camp ranger shall not investigate any cabin violations without the filing of a report from a cabin leader. Camp Tallawanda cabin leaders did not file reports about pranks, as a camp tradition. So, a prank could only be punished by a revenge prank.

* * *

It seemed everyone at camp had already heard about the attack by the time the Salamander cabin arrived for breakfast. Some of the sixth grade boys even laughed and stood up in the middle of the meal and ran around their table in a circle shouting to mock the seventh grade boys. Ricky face burned hot and red when he saw Zach Taylor talking over the eighth grade girl's table doing an impression of flailing motions with his arms.

"Look at that jerk," Ricky said to Marcus who sat next to him for the first time. During the scare, Ricky landed on Marcus when he jumped out of his bunk, but he helped Marcus get back up to his feet. The two of them ran out the door together, both falling down into the muck at the same time. But in that moment, before they knew it was a prank, thinking they were really trying to run for their lives, Ricky helped Marcus. It broke the ice.

"Listen guys," Heath said leaning into the table, and wiping his mouth. "I know you want to get them back for this prank, and you should."

All the cabin members nodded in approval so far with their leader.

"But I'm going to tell you right now, a prank will only feel good temporarily, but you guys really want to get them? You want to win the war?"

They whispered affirmatively.

"If you want to really beat these guys, you have to beat them in lacrosse."

All at once the huddle broke. The boys slid back and down into their chairs.

"Oh come on!" Heath said, trying to find eye contact with someone. "Great Dane? TJ? You guys don't want to beat them?"

"Of course we want to beat them," Spencer spoke for the group. "But news flash: they're really good."

"So what? They can't be that much better than you guys." Heath stayed positive. "They're only a year older. Ace, what do you say, you want to get even or do you want to win?"

"They're pretty good," Ace admitted.

"I don't believe you guys, don't you have any faith in yourselves?" Heath asked.

"I want to win," Ricky said, hardly louder than a whisper.

"You've never even played lacrosse," answered Dez.

"So what?" Ricky said, a little louder. "I came here cause TJ told me if I don't, I'd be a loser and now I'm here but you're all saying were going to be losers anyway? I want to win."

"Yeah," Heath nodded. "Ricky gets it."

"Ricky, came to camp, and only wants to win because of Hannah Havinghurst," TJ got the table to laugh.

"So what's wrong with being motivated?" Ricky blushed. "Who is going to teach me how to play lacrosse?"

The laughs brought the table together. The boys agreed they'd get their revenge on the eighth grade boys for pranking their cabin, but more importantly they vowed they'd have to challenge, and beat them in lacrosse. Ace and the rest of the cabin volunteered to help teach Ricky the game, and practice together to beat the eighth graders.

"Alright then," said Heath. "After breakfast, let's practice."

"Might as well practice, cause we ain't going on the blob," Dane shoved Spencer.

* * *

Ricky and the Salamander crew stood in the center of Cooke Field wearing all their equipment. Heath had black and white lacrosse gloves with a whistle around his neck. He dropped a bucket full of balls down on the ground in front of them. Ricky bent down holding his stick with two hands, one at the very top near the head, and the other at the very bottom end of the stick. He picked a ball up as if using his stick to dig a hole. Marcus and Dez both snatched a ball from the ground with only one hand at the very bottom of the handle of their stick.

"Keep practicin' Rick," Marcus teased.

"Ignore him, Ricky," said Heath. "Now show me how you cradle it."

"What does that mean?" Ricky asked.

"Are you kidding me!" laughed Artie from behind Heath.

Heath blew his whistle, and pointed at Artie, "Go take a lap."

"What for?"

"For giving your teammate a hard time about cradling." Heath threw a ball to Artie who caught it in his stick. "Now take a lap and cradle the ball the whole time." Heath blew his whistle two very short and hard times. "Let's go! Let's go!"

Artie hung his head as started his lap. Heath turned to the other boys from the cabin, "Well," he asked them.

"Well what?" Marcus replied.

"All of you grab a ball and go take a lap with Artie. Practice just started," he blew his whistle again. The team obeyed and chased after Artie, but Heath signaled for Ricky to stay behind.

"Alright Ricky, you see how all these guys are running with two hands on the stick?" Heath continued. "They got their bottom hand pretty loose and they bring the top of their stick down to their hip and curl their arm, like they're doing a bicep curl. That's cradling; you use the centrifugal force."

"Center-full what?" Ricky curled his stick up and down with his right arm while holding the bottom loosely in his left, trying to keep his left arm hanging straight.

"Centrifugal force. You ever twirl a bucket of water really fast around your head? The water doesn't fall out, right? That's called centrifugal force. Cradling forces the ball to stay nice and safe in the bottom of your pocket."

"Oh, I get it," Ricky had no idea what Heath was talking about, but he could tell the ball stayed in place.

"Now switch hands, cradle with your left arm."

"I don't know if I can," Ricky admitted. "It feels better with my right."

"Exactly," said Heath. "Any benchwarmer off the street can catch and throw with his right hand, but you're not a good lacrosse player until you can play with both. So you're going to learn as a lefty, and the right arm will come naturally."

As the words of Heath's first lesson sunk in, the boys came back from their lap.

"Alright, all you guys grab a partner. Get in a line, stand about 15 yards away from your partner and play catch. Ricky you stay with me."

"So this is practice? I already know how to catch," Said Great Dane. "We shoulda hit the pool instead of this."

Heath blew his whistle two times, loud and fast. "Take a lap, Dane."

"What? Why?" Dane pleaded.

"Because, if you want to learn how to be a good team, you have to learn how to work together, and it starts from the bottom up. Catching and throwing. Take a lap, big guy."

Heath gave the whistle two more hard and crisp blows. Dane swatted at the ball with his long stick, trying to mimic the way Marcus and Dez could snatch the ball up from the ground with one hand at the bottom of their stick, but gave up after several failed attempts.

"It's harder with the D-pole," Great Dane explained.

"Stop stalling and go," Heath turned to the rest of the players. "As a team. Hurry up!" Two more hard chirps from the whistle, and obeyed, again leaving Ricky and Heath alone to go over more of the basics.

"Alright Ricky. Time to catch and throw. Now, imagine the pocket of the stick is just an extension of your top hand. Imagine you are trying to catch the ball in your top hand, but it's just a little bit longer with the head of the stick poking out of it, okay?"

Heath threw the ball to Ricky and surprisingly, he caught it.

"It's not rocket science, it's lacrosse," Heath reminded Ricky.

"How do I throw it back?"

"Take your top hand, and slide to about midway down the stick. Stand with your right shoulder pointing to me, the way you would stand if you were going to throw me a football with your left hand."

"It feels weird as a lefty, can I just throw it right handed?" Ricky complained.

"Not on my watch. You have to learn both hands, so learn with the harder one first."

Ricky never played any kind of sport or anything left handed, every movement he made felt awkward and backwards, but he trusted Heath knew what it took to learn lacrosse.

"Cradle it back to behind your ear," Heath coached. "Put your top hand, your left hand, halfway down the stick. Stand with your right leg in front, aiming with your right foot towards me. Then, in one motion keeping your elbows up, imagine the stick is an extension of your arm, and throw me the ball, stepping through and finishing with your left foot forward, both feet and chest pointing to me."

Ricky readjusted his feet like a pitcher on a baseball mound. He pointed his right foot to Heath. He fidgeted with his hands a few times to make sure his grip was just right, everything felt weird trying to throw left-handed. He twisted his shoulders and chest towards Heath as he stepped into the throw with his left foot, and brought his arms through the motion, trying to pretend he wasn't holding the stick at all. The ball came out of his stick soaring too high, but it did go in Heath's general direction.

"Nice job, Ricky!" Heath said jogging after the ball. "You just need to work on that now, but not bad."

The other guys came jogging back in from their second lap.

"Okay, okay bring it in. Here's what we're going to do, Ricky, you see that brick shed?"

Ricky nodded.

"Go play catch with the wall, like how we talked about at dinner last week. Pick a brick, and aim to hit that brick. As for the rest of you: find a partner, we got work to do."

The cabin spent all morning practicing at Cooke Field. Heath had the boys going over ground ball drills, fast breaks, clearing, and face-offs. The whole time Ricky played catch with the wall. He seemed to be a natural at catching, but his throwing needed work. He could pick out a brick and manage to hit just within a few bricks of the target, but he never landed on the one he wanted to. Heath blew the whistle at around lunchtime, signaling Ricky to come back to the group.

"Listen up guys," Heath lectured. "95% of lacrosse is catching and passing. You got that? 95% of lacrosse is catching and passing, the other 15% is working harder than the other team."

"You got to give 110%?" Ricky suggested.

"I don't get it," Spencer said trying to do the math.

"Nerd alert," Great Dane answered.

"Remember," Heath raised his index finger. "Hard work beats talent, when talent doesn't work hard. You guys work together, and you work hard, you will beat the eighth graders. Good start today. Let's go to lunch."

CHAPTER 10

Crafting Creatively

"Of course I signed up for Outdoor Adventures," TJ scoffed in reply to Ricky's inquiry. "Everyone signed up for Outdoor Adventures. Didn't you?" The time for summer classes to start finally came. The first day of classes started on a Friday. This way, the campers could have an introduction, then enjoy their weekends. At breakfast, all the boys discussed where they'd be heading for the day.

Ricky put his head down and swirled his spoon around his cereal bowl, "No."

They all started laughing. Just when Ricky thought he had finally earned some respect from the guys, there it went, flying out the window when he told them his mom made him sign up for *Crafting Creatively.*

"What a loser," Spencer laughed; everyone else joined him.

"You going to be making doll houses?" Great Dane teased.

"He's probably going to be gluing popsicle stick cabins," Ben Li chimed in. Ben Li was one of the starting midfielders with Ace. He rarely spoke, but his dry humor always made the guys laugh; the popsicle comment brought plenty of giggles.

Ricky wanted to cry. What choice did he have? His parents wouldn't have let him come to camp if he didn't sign up for the class they picked. He could feel his face turning red, and his eyes started to tingle. When he hit the verge of bursting, Ricky heard from the seventh grade girls' table, the unmistakable voice of Hannah Havinghurst say, *"Crafting Creatively."* And all the other guys at the table heard it too, because all of them stopped laughing.

"Hey partner, might not be so bad," Ace give Ricky a light punch on the arm.

After breakfast, while the rest of the Salamander boys loaded up their water bottles to get ready to learn about the great outdoors, Ricky daydreamed about the girl with the ponytail. He stopped worrying about missing out on the fun in the explorer's class.

"Look at this guy," Marcus said pointing to Ricky. "The kid can't stop smiling."

Heath, who had just returned from his morning Cabin Leader's meeting, walked in to try and figure out what all the fuss was about.

"Ricky is the only one who has to take crafts class," TJ informed proudly.

"Ricky? Are you kidding me, dude?" Heath asked, in a polite, but insulting manner.

"It wasn't my choice," Ricky explained. "My parents forced me to take it."

"Still in the bubble," TJ shook his head.

"Good luck with that," Heath shrugged, then laughed a little too.

"That's all you got for me Heath?" Ricky pleaded. "Mister I-Know-Everything just tells me good luck? Come on man"

The rest of the Salamander guys joined in, eager to hear their cabin leader impart wisdom on meeting girls.

Heath scratched his chin and said, "I'll tell ya what..." He loved to pause for dramatic effect. "You don't go after either of the two cutest girls in the room; you want the third cutest girl in the room."

"That makes zero sense," Dez winced his red eyebrows together.

"Because," Heath went on, "The two prettiest girls aren't ever as pretty as they think they are."

"Oh, what do you know?" Spencer waived off Heath's advice.

"You all might be a little too young to listen, but the prettiest girl in the room isn't funny, and she's not good at anything; all she cares about is being the prettiest girl in the room."

"What about the second prettiest girl in the room?" Ben Li asked.

"Lost cause," Heath grunted. "She only cares about competing with the prettiest one. And trust me guys, pretty doesn't last long."

"We're twelve years old, dude," Artie pointed out. "It'll last awhile."

"I don't know about that, Heath," TJ hesitated. "Hannah's pretty hot, so is her mom."

"Maybe," Heath admitted. "But, I bet you there's cuter girls at this camp that are cool and fun, and don't care so much about being popular. Look for them; that's my advice."

Ricky mulled over Heath's words for a minute, than asked, "Yeah, but, what if I *do* want the cutest girl in the room? Then what?"

Heath laughed with the rest of the cabin at Ricky's honesty, "Young and dumb. Okay. You want the popular girl to like you?"

"Yea he does!" TJ answered for the suddenly shy new kid.

"Then, you got to sit next to her," Heath said calm and slow.

The whole cabin gasped.

"What? No way; I'm not doing that," Ricky protested. "Then she's going to know I like her!"

"It's the only way, young grasshopper." Heath said. "Think about it: it's arts class, right? You're going to be working with partners. You want this girl to like you? Talk to her. How you going to talk to her? Be her partner. If you don't, some other guy whose parents wanted to make him miserable is going to ask her, and you're out."

Heath made some good points.

Ricky nodded, "Okay... okay. I'll do it."

"No he won't," Spencer insisted.

"You too scared," Great Dane sneered.

"No, I'm serious," Ricky said standing up. "I'll do it. I'm going to walk in there and I'm plopping down right next to Hannah, and nothing's gonna stop me."

"Ricky man, no you ain't," Ace predicted.

* * *

Ricky walked up to the schoolhouse determined he'd sit next to Hannah, or at least, he'd muster up enough courage to ask her to be his partner. Worrying about how he'd ask her, he forgot how to walk and almost sprained his ankle walking up the steps. Hopefully, nobody saw him lose his footing.

Inside the one-room redbrick schoolhouse, long rows of wooden desks sat on top of cast iron legs screwed to the ground. The campers sat on long wooden benches, polished to a smooth slippery finish. The room had high ceilings, and similar antler chandeliers to the ones in the Grand Hall. The schoolhouse smelled of old air that made its way in many years ago, and settled down into a corner somewhere. But, Ricky didn't notice any of the details of the classroom. His eyes focused on one thing and one thing only: Hannah. And sitting right next to her, with a head full of gelled spiked hair, was Zach Taylor.

"You've got to be kidding me," Ricky whispered to himself. His stomach dropped down to his knees. It wasn't just Zach; the other big bully defender, whatever his name was, Patrick Winker-something, and the goalie, Nolan Stier were there too. Hannah and her tall skinny friend Kristin sat sandwiched between the goons with Zach in the middle of the girls. Ricky had no chance. He shook his head, lowered it, and slid into the back row of seats, alone.

Wait till the guys hear about this one, he shuddered.

Someone sat down in the seat next to him, but Ricky was too dejected to notice. He focused on trying to eavesdrop on Zach and his friends about how genius and honorable it was of them to take a crafting class.

"Oh sure," Zach bragged. "We did the outdoors class last year, and it's a lot of fun and all, but we noticed there were no guys in the crafts class. So, we figured we'd come give you girls some company."

Ricky rolled his eyes.

"That's so cool of you," Hannah said blushing.

"Um yeah," Kristin stuck her pointy chin out and tilted her head to one side. "Like, I think it's like so brave."

Urgh, Ricky groaned to himself. *How can they believe this stuff?*

"It is brave," Nolan, added. Ricky thought Nolan actually gained weight since the scrimmage just a couple days ago. Ricky could see the fat rolls showing from the polka-dot shirt suctioned onto Nolan's body. "We're man enough to admit we like arts and crafts," the eighth grade goalie bragged.

"Oh pa-leez," said the feminine voice sitting next to Ricky. Ricky turned to see that it belonged to the curly haired blonde girl, the one he saw on his way to the lacrosse game.

"Hey there," she chomped out from her chewing gum. "I'm Claire Minnich."

Ricky reached out to shake Claire's hand, and hoped she didn't notice that he once again tried sneaking a peek in Hannah's direction. Claire did notice, but she ignored it.

"What's your name?" she asked.

"Ricky Collins."

"Ricky huh?" Claire strained her eyes staring at him. Then she asked, "Are you going to tell me you took the arts and crafts class to get in touch with your inner artist too?"

"No, not exactly," Ricky scratched the back of his head, unsure how he should explain this one. "My parents kind of forced me to sign up for this instead of the outdoors class."

Probably not like that.

"Why?" Claire chomped.

"I don't know. They always think something terrible is going to happen to me all the time. They said if I didn't sign up for this class, they wouldn't let me come to camp at all."

"Are they crazy or something?"

Ricky thought about his answer, "No not really. I think they're just trying to make sure I turn out to be."

Claire rocked back in her chair, and gave Ricky a flirtatious back handed swat while she laughed at his joke. When she finished laughing she leaned forward, looking at him with attentive ears. She waited for him to say something else, but Ricky had nothing prepared.

"This is my first year at camp," he blurted out.

"Yeah I know. You were in my sixth grade class for one day, everybody knows. But don't worry, it won't be too bad. I heard we're making wooden lacrosse sticks."

"Is everything at this camp about lacrosse?" Ricky asked.

"You don't like lacrosse?"

"No, I do," he said. "I just didn't really play it that much in my old town." And although he didn't dare say it, he thought, *I've never even heard about it in my whole life.*

"I love lacrosse," Claire assured him. "I've been playing for years."

"Girls can play lacrosse too?" Ricky had no idea.

"Yeah, and I betchya I'm better than you," Claire said stone-face serious.

The class teacher, a camp ranger, entered. She wore the same high socks and drill sergeant hat like the other camp rangers. She introduced herself as Camp Ranger Gladys.

She announced that their current seats would be their permanent seats for the summer. This way she could learn everyone's names.

"Hope we get along," Claire winked.

"Me too," Ricky glanced at Zach and Hannah.

After Ranger Gladys had the students go around the room to introduce themselves, she said that their summer partners would be the person sitting next to them. Within two minutes of walking through the door, Ranger Gladys destroyed any and all hopes Ricky had of talking to Hannah for the whole summer. His parents would have been impressed. But, being partnered with the outgoing Claire Minnich made him wonder if Heath's theory would prove true.

* * *

Back at the cabin, TJ, Spencer, Ace, and the rest of the guys had the pleasure of telling Ricky about how much fun he was missing out on in Outdoor Adventures. Great Dane bragged about how the camp ranger took them up the trail towards a mountain. Artie explained how the boys would be learning to tie ropes, start fires, and even get to hike along the outer edges of the campgrounds. They asked Ricky if he sat next to Hannah, and he had to tell them that he didn't. After those laughs subsided, he had to admit that the class did split up into partners. But again, no, he didn't get partnered with Hannah. And finally, no, he didn't say a word to her. Yes, just like they told him he wouldn't. Ricky decided he had been picked on enough for the day, and chose not to tell them about Claire. When the guys asked him why he didn't sit next to Hannah, he told them it was because of Zach Taylor. Something needed to be done about Porcupine cabin.

CHAPTER 11

Salamanders v. Falcons

On Saturday morning, Ricky, TJ, and Great Dane were standing in line when Claire and her friends approached them. Unlike Hannah and Kristin, Claire and her friends wore one-piece bathing suits. Ricky tried to keep his eyes on the girls' faces.

"Hey Ricky," Claire waived.

Dane shot a surprising look over at TJ.

"Hey Claire, this is TJ and Dane."

"We all know each other from school," Claire reminded the new kid. "Ricky this is Paige Bacco, and Danielle Camina; everyone here knows everybody except you."

"But they never talk to us," the petite Danielle said putting a hand on her hip. A purple clip kept her wet hair away from her face.

"Ricky, are these your friends from crafts class?" TJ joked.

"Instead of being on the zip line shouldn't you guys be practicing?" Paige asked Dane. Paige was tall for age, taller than Ricky, but she had thin limbs and long fingers with green painted nails.

"What's that s'posed to mean?" Dane replied.

"You're going to re-match the eighth graders aren't you? From what I heard, you need some practice," Danielle explained.

"Don't you girls got your own beef to worry 'bout?" Great Dane argued. "Heard you're challenging the eighth grade girls soon."

TJ stood aloof with his body turned slightly away from the conversation and his arms crossed to be as rude and uninterested as possible.

"That's why we came over here," Paige said checking the time on her sports watch. "Would you guys want to come practice with us after lunch?"

"Why would we want to play with you?" asked TJ without turning his shoulders.

"Are you scared we'll beat you?" Claire pressed. "The eighth grade girls are practicing with the eighth grade boys, we thought it might be fun," she spoke to Ricky for support.

"I don't know anything about the rules for girls lacrosse," Ricky said luring TJ into the conversation.

TJ turned his body fully towards the group, "I'm not afraid. I don't think playing with the girls is going to be fun, that's all."

"I kind of do," Ricky said looking at Claire, but thinking about how it would be a great way to finally talk to Hannah.

"Might be," said Dane. "You know you want to showoff, TJ. Admit it."

"We'd probably win 100 to zero," TJ boasted. Then he checked out Danielle in her floral patterned bathing suit, "But it could be fun."

"Yeah, it will," said Danielle, looking TJ right in the eye.

"Okay, then we'll see you at Cooke Field after lunch," Claire smiled at Ricky.

* * *

When Salamander cabin arrived at Cooke Field, they found the girls there already warming up. Both cabins brought full attendance. Which meant Brittney was there too; Heath thanked himself for tagging along.

"What are they wearing?" Ricky asked referring to the strange looking goggles the girls had on their heads.

"You really don't know anything about lacrosse," said Artie. "It's their goggles. Girls don't wear helmets, except the goalie, because they aren't allowed to hit each other."

"No way they can see outta those things," Ricky figured.

"Look at that," Spencer pointed at cabin leader Brittney. Brittney wore no socks or kneepads, exposing her athletic legs and skinny ankles. Ricky wondered where someone could even buy shorts so short.

"Don't stare too long," Ace warned. "Like starin' at the sun."

Ricky finally caught sight of Hannah. Of all the girls, only Hannah and Kristin wore makeup. He winced a little thinking about how gross it would be to have makeup sweat down into her eyes. Claire stood in the back near Brittney, she didn't wear any makeup, but she used a pink ribbon to tie her curly hair.

"Keep your tongues in your mouths guys," Heath suggested. "Let's jog it in."

The way Heath kept fiddling with the whistle hanging from his neck, Ricky could tell he was nervous and that he liked Brittney. Technically, every guy in Salamander had a crush on Brittney, but Heath had a real crush. They voted unanimously to play boys versus girls, and they'd play using the girls' field lines. Brittney also insisted that the boys' defenders use regular short sticks, of course Heath agreed.

"What about face-offs?" Brittney asked.

"You girls can start with the ball every time," Heath conceded.

"What!" TJ shouted.

"Not fair!" argued Great Dane.

The rest of the boys joined in with their disapproval.

"What, are you scared you're going to lose?" asked Karen Laund, the girls' goalie. Karen was what Ricky's mother would call a *handsome girl*. She had large shoulders, a wide foundation, and curly maroon hair.

"Take it easy guys," Heath stepped in just in time to cut off Spencer from opening his mouth with what was undoubtedly going to be a vicious rebuttal aimed at Karen.

"Take it easy," Heath repeated. "Spencer. We're just trying to have a friendly game and give you all a chance to get to know each other a little. Brittney, are you okay with us both coaching and refereeing at the same time?"

"Yeah, I think that's a good idea," Brittney winked. "Anyone here got any other questions?"

"Are we playing shirts and skins?" Spencer giggled.

Brittney rolled her eyes, "Any *real* questions?"

"What does the winner get?" Ben Li asked.

The weight of the question fell equally on all ears, followed by a long silence. At first, probably everyone thought *a kiss*. But, nobody had the guts to suggest it, not even Spencer. The uneasy silence lingered while everyone looked around wondering whom they'd pick to get or give their prize.

"How about automatic cuts in line anywhere in camp?" Brittney suggested. The response brought cheers from boys and girls alike. It was an acceptable alternative, at least.

"Alright, Heath. Get your team on the other sideline, and get your starters ready to go."

Ricky drastically improved his lacrosse game. He practiced constantly, and his dedication showed. But he wasn't good enough to be a starter. Claire on the other hand, started at attack, or *home*, as he learned girls called the position. While Claire jogged to her spot on the field, Hannah sat at the very end of the bench with Kristin. They slouched on the bench talking with their legs crossed, and their goggles up on their foreheads.

Little Danielle Camina in mismatched knee socks started with the ball at the midfield. Nobody wanted to be the guy who whacked a girl with his lacrosse stick, so they gave the girls too much distance. The Falcons easily moved the ball down into their offensive zone. Claire worked her way behind the goal without the ball while Dane did his best to cover her. Dane wasn't used to playing defense with a short stick, or giving an opponent so much space. So, when Claire made a juke step, she got past him quickly and drove forward. Paige passed it straight into her stick. Claire planted her front foot, twisted her hips, and in one motion fired the ball out with an accurate side-arm throw. Somehow, Spencer blocked the shot.

"Aw crap!" Claire shouted and hustled into position to cover the clear with a smile.

"Claire's pretty good," Artie admired from the sidelines to Ricky.

"Yeah, she is," Ricky nodded.

"Is she your girlfriend?" Artie probed.

"No way, dude," Ricky shrugged off the question.

"Why not?"

Ricky thought about it as he watched Hannah braid her hair on the bench, "I'm not sure."

After blocking Claire's shot, Spencer started to run the ball out from the goal. None of the guys were surprised he wanted to show-off. Danielle ran over to cover him, but he spun around her.

"Oh man, I think he's going to try and score," Artie chuckled.

Another girl came up to try and get the ball out of Spencer's stick but he dipped under her and took a side shuffle step to continue his way down the field. Spencer looked like a superstar at this point, and everyone realized he'd attempt the very rare goalie goal.

"Slide over! Slide over!" Karen shouted from her goalie spot.

Spencer dipped under a final Falcon cabin defender and took a mammoth swing at the goal. His shot went straight into the pocket of Karen's stick.

"Oops," Spencer gulped; he left the boys' net completely unattended.

Without hesitation, Karen wound up and launched the ball into the air. There was nothing anyone, especially Spencer, could do but watch Karen's shot soar overhead into the wide-open goal on the other end of the field. The girls ran to their goalie to join in a group hug and celebration. Spencer had to jog back to his post with his head down.

"Spencer, you're a scrub!" shouted Marcus.

"Why'd you do that?" Dez asked holding both of his palms out to his sides. "We're all wide open, ya fool!"

"Oh chill out! It's one goal," Spencer said with his tail between his legs.

"That was one of the stupidest things I've ever seen," TJ laughed.

"Get back to your spots," Spencer snapped.

"Idiot!" Great Dane barked.

When Claire saw Ricky coming in to sub for Ben Li, she went up to take the faceoff.

"Look who's finally playing lacrosse," she said to Ricky.

"How many goals have you scored?" he joked back.

Claire sprinted towards Ricky, her pink ribbon bobbing with each step. He had to back peddle full speed stay in front of her. She pulled up, stopping right on a dime, and switched her cradling to the opposite hand. *She's really good,* Ricky said to himself. Claire took a few more steps, and then passed it towards the bottom of the crease to Paige. When Paige tried to pass it back to Claire over Ricky's head, he reached up to intercept it. The ball bounced off the edge of his stick but rolled straight to TJ. TJ scooped it up and the boys went running down the field to play offense.

TJ passed the ball to Ace, and Ace heaved it all the way down to Dez. Dez passed it back immediately straight into Ricky's stick. He had a wide-open lane to the goal. Ricky took an underhand shot that went through Karen's knees and into the back of the net.

"Oh yeah!" he shouted pointing at Claire.

Ricky received high-fives from Ace, Marcus, Dez and the rest of the boys on offense. He smiled to himself jogging back to the line. He looked over on the sidelines, Hannah and Kristin hadn't moved from the bench. They had no idea Ricky scored, or even that a game was going on at all. Claire, she shook her head, but gave Ricky a thumbs up.

"Go back to the sidelines," Claire suggested.

Ricky needed to catch his breath from sprinting, so he went back to the bench. Artie greeted him with a high-five and his water bottle. Ricky took a swig, then looked back at Claire. She was still looking at him, and they locked eyes for a half-second. Artie noticed.

"Wow man," Artie crossed his hands over his heart. "You've got a girlfriend and you don't even know it . . . It ain't no Hannah Havinghurst either."

Ricky smiled but didn't reply.

After the next possession, Hannah and Kristin were forced to sub into the game. Hannah didn't look so cute anymore wearing her goggles, and she kept laughing. Kristin took the free face-off, holding her sick out in front of her like a waitress carrying a tray of dishes. As soon the boy defender got close, she tried throwing it over to Hannah. The ball only made it about half the distance before it bounced off the ground. Instead of trying to catch it, Hannah shrieked and picked one leg up to cover her body from the ball. It rolled past her, and Ace scooped it up and ran down the field. A few good passes later, Marcus scored.

"Jeez, Hannah sucks," Artie said to Ricky. "She's hot, but she sucks."

"I'm starting to think so too," Ricky sighed.

As the scrimmage went on, the boys pulled away on the scoreboard. The final score was 13-4. Brittney thanked Heath for helping the girls get ready for their big game against the eighth grade girls. Spencer made sure to remind the girls that the boys would get to cut in front of them at the zip line.

"You're pretty good out there," Ricky smirked, "for a girl."

"Yeah, you're weren't terrible," Claire shrugged, "for a rookie."

"See ya in class," he said turning away.

"Later," Claire said back.

But the two turned in the same direction. Goosebumps ran all the way up from Ricky's shins to his stomach and chest with uneasiness. *Should I say something else?* He wondered. Luckily, Ace called Ricky over to the group of the others. He half-turned his shoulders towards her twice, but in that brief moment decided not to say anything and jogged away, regretting the whole thing.

Hannah and Kristin walked by Ricky and the other guys, making sure to not even glance in their direction. Hannah's makeup was still fresh on her face, because she didn't sweat, or try, or care at all about lacrosse. Ricky began to see what Heath tried to tell him.

CHAPTER 12

"Are you eating?"

"Mr. Richard Collins?" a khaki clad, knee socks wearing camp ranger asked holding his clipboard over the Salamander cabin's lunch table.

"Yes?"

"Your parents requested a phone call with you. Please come with me after you're finished eating to the Commissioner's Office."

"Can't I just call them from the rec-room phones?" Ricky asked.

"If a parent requests a phone call, it has to be made from the Commissioner's Office. Camp Tallawanda policy. I'll be rounding up a few other campers, and we'll go together." He spun around on the heel of his mountain hiking boots and looked down at his clipboard before walking over to another lunch table to find his next camper to bear the bad news.

They had to go all the way to the back end of the campground to get to the Commissioner's Office. Luckily, the camp ranger let Ricky and the three other campers ride along in his double-row golf cart to get there. The single floor ranch cabin had bright orange shutters with a matching highlighter orange front door.

The inside of the Commissioner's Office looked like a mix between a sports lodge, a principal's office, and a tree fort. Wooden lacrosse sticks, trophies and camp memorabilia decorated every wall. Pictures on the wall dated as far as the camp's first year, with only a handful of campers in black and white photos. There were pictures of Fort Tallawanda, when the camp was a fort for soldiers during the Civil War era. Pictures from that time showed cowboys sitting around a bonfire. Ricky laughed at pictures of young boys from about forty years ago wearing lacrosse helmets and equipment. Their old helmets looked like horse jockey helmets with football facemasks screwed into them.

The receptionist sat in front of an ancient desktop computer wearing thick reading glasses that hung from an old chain, and an old knit grandma sweater around her shoulders. The peculiar thing about her was that although she dressed like a grandma, she couldn't have been more than a couple years older than Heath. She tied her hair up on the top of her head with a pencil and a pen sticking out from opposite sides, and pounded and popped on blue bubble gum.

"You Richard Collins?" she asked.

"Ricky, yeah."

"We don't like to have to make you call your parents, kid," she blew a big blue bubble until it popped. "It's not fun for anyone. Try and give Mom a call next time from the rec room, okay?"

She pointed Ricky to the Phone Booth area the way a flight attendant points to the exit signs on a plane. Ricky started walking down that direction. The six phone booths stood in a line at the end of the hall. They looked like the classic red ones from England.

"You know your phone number, kid?" she asked chomping on her gum.

"Yeah," Ricky knew the question was an insult.

"Too bad," she chewed. "I coulda given you mine."

"What?" he turned around to ask her, but she started stacking papers on her desk.

She hunched over, focusing all her attention on making sure the papers were exactly even before stapling them together. She stapled them, then swirled around in her chair and threw them in what seemed like a random file cabinet behind her. She never looked back at Ricky.

"Is this Ricky?" his mother asked as she picked up the phone. "Ricky, I've been worried sick about you. Where have you been? You haven't called in days. Have you been eating?"

"Yes. I know. I just got busy up here, there's a lot going on,"

"Too busy to call your own mother? We send you up to camp and you don't call us anymore?"

"Mom, I'm sorry, I was going to call you tomorrow. Things get really busy during the day and I kept forgetting, and the phones are only in the rec room."

"Do all the other boys forget to call their mothers? I was about to have the police come looking for you. Have you been eating? How's the food up there?"

"Yeah, I've been eating. It's good."

"Better than mine? How much are you eating? I don't want you coming back like a string bean. Are they making you lunches? I'll send you some sandwiches. Do you want any sandwiches?"

Ricky threw his head back and looked up to the ceiling with a hand over his forward. He was hours away from his parent's house, but he felt like he was sitting at the kitchen table being scolded by them. He could hear his father in the background making commentary. *This is why I haven't been calling*, he reminded himself.

"Ask him if he's made any friends," he heard his dad say.

Ricky could picture the scene exactly at his parents' house: Mom sitting at the kitchen table in her pink sweatshirt, with her feet resting on the chair next to her, unconsciously shaking her foot so as to never be relaxed. Dad was at the kitchen counter, probably standing over a stack of mail, trying to read the letters through the envelope by holding them up to the light; or transferring the contents of two half empty bags of cereal into a third nearly empty bag. He did this to conserve space in the cabinets that always had plenty of space.

"Of course he's making friends, Dale. Ricky, Dad wants to know if you've made any friends; tell him you've made friends."

"I didn't say he couldn't make friends, Marsh. I just wanted to know if he did," Mr. Collins argued.

"Well, he hasn't called us. What do you think he's been doing up there? Of course he's made friends."

"I wanted to know if he's spending all his time up there with that Stanton kid," Mr. Collins clarified.

"Helllllooo?" Ricky interrupted his parent's argument to remind them they were still on the phone with him.

"You aren't spending all your time with TJ are you?" his mother asked, and before Ricky could answer, she continued. "There's lots of other kids you can be hanging out with up there, you know? We met the Lutz family the other weekend; they seem very nice. You should spend more time with Spencer."

"And stay away from girls!" his dad yelled.

"We didn't send you up there to be courting any girls, you know?"

"Yeah, okay. I know, Mom," Ricky closed his eyes and pinched his nose.

"Did you tell him we're coming?" he heard his father ask, over the sound of ripping cardboard boxes.

They're coming? Ricky gasped to himself feeling nauseous.

"I'm getting to that, Dale. I wanted to make sure he's alive first."

"Of course he's alive."

"Helllloooo!" Ricky had to break up the argument again.

"Your father and I are coming to visit," his mother relayed.

"What? Why? ... I mean, when?"

"The weekend before parent's weekend."

"Why don't you just come up for parent's weekend?" Ricky worried.

"Oh, we are." Mrs. Collins explained. "But we called the camp, and we're coming the weekend before parent's weekend, too. Isn't that exciting?"

"My heart is racing just thinking about it," Ricky admitted.

"We'll be there in a few weeks, I'm so excited to see you. Do you miss us?"

"How can he miss us? He never calls," Mr. Collins called out in the background.

"He's been busy, Dale! Of course he misses us."

The conversation with his parents went on like this for a few more minutes. His mother asked and answered a few more of her own questions, until finally Ricky said he had to go. The Collins's exchanged I-love-you's and hung up. Ricky had to take a few deep breaths before walking out of the phone booth. The receptionist was on the phone. She held the outdated handset between her shoulder and her ear while typing furiously. Ricky could have sworn she winked at him while he walked towards the exit.

"Let me put you on hold real quick," she said to the other end of the line. Then she slammed down the phone and hung up on them.

"How'd it go in there?" she asked.

"Fine," Ricky shrugged. "Is anyone going to give me a ride back to the cabin?"

"Sorry big guy: don't talk, gotta walk." She definitely winked at him this time. "Remember to call your parents from the rec room."

Then she slammed one hand on the back of the phone, popping it up into the air and catching it simultaneously as it just uttered the first sounds of a ring. The receptionist swiveled in her chair, turning her back to Ricky and started right where she left off with whoever it was on the other end of the phone.

CHAPTER 13

North America's First Sport

Although Ricky didn't want his weekend of practicing lacrosse and riding go-karts to end, he looked forward to seeing Claire in crafting class on Monday morning. He showed up early and had to watch Zach, Patrick What's-his-name, and Nolan stroll in with Hannah and Kristin sandwiched in between them as always. The girls had so much makeup on their faces they looked like they should be going to an awards ceremony.

Claire staggered in a little late with Danielle and Paige. Claire wore no makeup, but kept her curly blonde hair well groomed and smelling like a garden.

"What are those dingbats talking about now?" she asked Ricky as she sat down.

"Hey. Just the normal, '*Oh Zach Taylor, you're the best,*' routine," Ricky reported.

"Don't be so jealous," Claire said wagging a finger in his face. "There's more important things in life than worrying about whether someone you don't care about cares about you."

"Like what? Lacrosse?" Ricky suggested.

"Yeah exactly. By the way, you're pretty fast out there," Claire blushed.

"Thanks. You're really good too."

"I said you're fast Ricky, didn't say anything about good," she smiled.

Ricky let out a sound combining a single laugh, a cough and a sigh.

"That first shot you took, that was pretty good," he continued.

"Urgh, I'm so mad Spencer blocked that. How hilarious was that goal Karen scored though?"

"The guys teased him all weekend for it," Ricky laughed.

"Hey new kid," Karen Laund said, as she lumbered towards her desk. "Lucky shot."

"Thanks? Yours too. We were just talking about it."

"Spencer's an idiot," she said and turned to take her seat.

Ranger Gladys stomped into class holding a wooden lacrosse stick.

"Pipe down, pipe down everyone," Ranger Gladys speed walked to front of the room. "Good morning. Well, enough with the small talk, isn't it? Let's get started, okay. Does anyone know what this is?" she held a wooden lacrosse stick. "This is a traditional lacrosse stick. We are going to learn the history of lacrosse this week. And then, we're going to learn how to string a wooden stick."

"Do we get to keep the sticks?" someone asked without raising her hand.

"Of course you'll be keeping your sticks."

The room filled with the ear piercing elation of a room full of girls.

"But we'll never get to stringing them with all these interruptions. May we begin?"

Ranger Gladys pressed a button and a presentation screen rolled down on the blackboard. It was time for a movie. The static in the background, the intro music, and the low-quality graphic of the title page, hinted that it was going to be an educational documentary. Camp Tallawanda had a strict policy designed to minimize electronics, so this was the first kind of TV any of the campers had contact with in weeks. The room was all too eager to stare mindlessly at whatever was going to come on the video screen.

The film's narrator spoke over the electronic music. "Join us today for," and then the fuzzy computer 2-D words appeared: "The Beginnings of North America's First Sport: Lacrosse."

The host's outfit suggested that the documentary must have been from right around the time Ricky's parents were in high school. The camera started with a wide shot and zoomed in on the speaker walking through a park, wearing a mustard brown sports coat and tight grey slacks. He had a thick mustache and a comb-over haircut, he was holding a modern-day lacrosse stick; well, modern for the time the video was filmed.

"In today's lesson, we'll discuss what we know about the game of lacrosse," the host explained. "We'll cover the history of its clouded past, and the widespread growth for boys and girls today. Join me as we embark on this journey."

Ricky found the scenes showing a reenactment of the 1600's depicting how Native Americans first played the game to be the most interesting. The dramatization showed what looked like 100 men running around carrying wooden poles with strange rounded nets at the top of them. Men in war paint tossed a strange looking ball around a giant field. Supposedly, this was how explorers first described the earliest lacrosse games.

The documentary said that Native Americans played lacrosse long before any European settlers arrived. According to historians, it seemed that most of the Eastern tribes in North America played some version of the same game. In some cultures, the name translated meaning, "to bump hips," in others it meant, "ball and stick," and in some tribes they called the game, "little brother of war." Ricky had no idea lacrosse was such an old sport.

Historically, Native Americans considered the game sacred. Some believed it was a gift passed down to them from their Creator. The original games would begin with feasts and rituals, and could last several days with hundreds of men playing at once. If two tribes had a dispute with each other, instead of going to battle, they could choose to play lacrosse. They'd agree that the winner of the game would also win the dispute and the spoils of war.

Eventually, the European settlers learned how to play. Lacrosse got its name from the French; it means "the stick." By the 1890's, both men and women were playing organized lacrosse games. Colleges on the east coast started to have lacrosse teams. Lacrosse even used to be in the Olympics during the early 1900's. As its popularity spread, more and more colleges had teams for both men and women.

The sports broadcaster explained that the reason lacrosse is so popular in modern times is because athletes of all difference shapes, sizes, and skillsets can play. Big athletes play with strength and power, smaller and more agile athletes play the game with finesse and ball handling skills, and the bravest souls play goalie. Girl's lacrosse doesn't allow much contact, but it is one of the toughest and fastest sports to play. For boys, the rules offer the contact of football, the speed of hockey, the endurance of soccer, and the transition scoring like basketball.

Finally, the video talked about the lacrosse stick. In the earliest days, sticks looked all sorts of different shapes and sizes. The most common traditional wooden stick was made out of one single piece of wood. Some cultures still use the same style in present day. The video ended with the sports anchor explaining that although the sticks have changed to become made of metal and plastic, the game still has ties to its cultural roots, and continues to grow more popular every year.

Before he moved next door to TJ, Ricky didn't know the game of lacrosse existed. But from the moment he put on those black and powder blue gloves, he knew he liked it. Finding out the game was a thousand years old blew his mind. Now, Ricky loved lacrosse.

Ranger Gladys stood up and turned off the projector.

"That's all the time we have for today, class. Tomorrow, we start working on our sticks."

CHAPTER 14

Don't Let Go!

At the lunch table, Ricky retold everything he could remember from the documentary, which was practically every word. Dane and Dez claimed they knew the game started from Native Americans. But none of them knew anything about the history of the sticks. Ricky couldn't wait for them to finish lunch and begged them to practice instead of going to the high ropes course, like they had planned.

"We're going to the high ropes course, dude," TJ said.

"What about re-matching Porcupine cabin?" Ricky pleaded. "We need practice."

"Nobody cares about those porcupine pricks right now," Spencer waived off Ricky's plea.

"The high ropes course is a team building activity," Ben Li explained. "Technically, it is practice."

"Sorry partner, Heath's on high ropes course duty this week," Ace put his hand on Ricky's shoulder. "We ain't gonna miss his first day."

"Fine," Ricky sighed. "Can we practice after?"

"I'll let you practice taking shots when we get back," Spencer said.

"Because you need improvement after all the girls scored on you?" Ben Li asked with such a straightforward face nobody knew if he was being insulting or sincere.

"Yeah," Spencer admitted to the laughter of the whole table.

* * *

Despite the glaring afternoon sun, the giant pine trees surrounding the high ropes course kept the area cool. High above them, various cables and wires stretched from tree to tree. The cables, which were connected to tree trunks, rope ladders, bars, and steps, spread out across the forest ceiling. When the Salamander squad arrived, they were happily surprised to see Flacon cabin leader Brittney was also assigned to high-ropes duty.

"Jackpot," Artie whispered to the group.

"That's the luckiest tank-top in the world," Spencer said without blinking.

"No wonder Heath was in such a good mood all morning," TJ scoffed.

"Hey Salamanders," Brittney waived.

The two cabin leaders had just finished setting up the gear before the boys arrived. Heath and Brittney already had their harnesses and red helmets on, and instructed the Salamander boys to grab one of each. Brittney laughed as the guys struggled with their harnesses. She held the black nylon straps up and explained how the loop with the blue tape went in the front, and the red tape on the loop was for the right leg. Despite the instructions, the boys couldn't figure it out.

"How the heck do you put this on?" Marcus asked tangled in the straps hopping on one foot.

"Oh man this is squeezing my nuts!" Artie screeched while trying to cram his plump body through a leg loop.

"Mine don't feel right," Ace complained.

"Dude," Brittney laughed. The boys never heard a college girl say *dude* before. "You've got it on backwards."

Brittney dropped to one knee to assist him. Watching her unstrap Ace's harness, and help him put it back on properly, made the others regret they hadn't put their harnesses on backwards too. Ace raised his eyebrows and smirked to the group while Brittney adjusted the straps around his thighs.

"I think I need some help too," TJ suggested, unable to mask the deception in his voice.

"Nice try, pal," Brittney shook her head. "Okay, everyone follow me and Health up this ladder to the top of the fort."

With their harnesses secured, and helmets buckled, they climbed the fifteen-foot ladder to the starting point. Heath and Brittney went through the safety spiel. Brittney demonstrated how each harness had two safety clips and that throughout the course the boys would have to transfer from one line to another.

"Guys, this is the most important part: you have to make sure you have one clip connected to the ropes at all times, okay?" she made eye-contact with each of them. "This is to make sure nobody falls and dies," she added half-joking.

"Has anyone ever died?" Ricky asked.

"Not on my watch," said Heath.

"You've done this zero times," Spencer pointed out.

The first obstacle was a balance beam about 20 feet long. A small thin cable stretched across, about waist high, which the boys latched their safety clips to as instructed. Brittney said they could let out slack on their safety straps, so it wouldn't feel like they weren't clipped in at all. But, she warned, the longer the slack, the more it would yank on the harness if they did fall. Most of the boys, including Ricky, let the slack out all the way. The first board was about a foot-wide, and the brave Salamanders had no trouble sprinting across to the checkpoint.

The tightrope walk wasn't as easy. The slack in the rope made it wobbly; everyone had to cling to the chest-high cable as a stabilizer. The ground seemed to be about a mile away. Ricky imagined falling, and wondered if he'd die instantly, or survive the landing with a mutilated body. How much would it hurt if he broke all his arms and legs? He tightened his grip on the assistance cable and focused on shuffling his feet across one step at a time.

"You're doing good guys; you got this!" Brittney shouted support as they inched across the tightrope.

Artie was very obviously scared: he only moved his feet about three inches at a time and held on to the safety rope with his elbows. His fists turned blue from squeezing so hard.

"Hurry up out there, Art," Great Dane barked. Dane had already made it across, and grabbed on to the safety cable and started shaking it.

"Stop! Stop!" Artie shrieked with panic on his snow-white face.

"Okay guys, settle down," Britney said, holding back her laughter.

"Stop being such a baby, Artie," TJ joked.

Eventually, Artie made it across the tight rope, and the boys advanced to the next obstacle. After climbing up the rope ladder, they were about 40-feet up in the strong ponderosa trees. Ricky's hands were bleeding, and a few of them had scrapes on their knees, or scratches on their stomachs from the harnesses.

"Okay Salamanders, this part is called the Spy Crawl," explained Brittney. "We're going to hook your safety harnesses up along this wire and you hang upside-down and crawl across this rope, got it?"

"That looks impossible," Dez gulped.

"No, its not. I'll go first," Heath encouraged them.

The leader hooked himself into the overhead safety wire, then reached his arms overhead and swung his feet up to wrap his ankles around the rope. Heath crept his hands and his ankles over about a foot at a time. When he got to the midway point, with nothing between him and the ground 40 feet below, the boys all double checked to make sure their harnesses were secure.

"Who is going next?" Brittney asked.

"I don't think this is such a good idea for a big guy," Artie trembled.

"Oh come on, you'll be fine; let some more of your friends go first, and you'll see it isn't so bad," Brittney reassured him.

Dane, Ace, and TJ all managed to make it across without any issues. Then Ricky and the rest of the cabin successfully completed the spy crawl. Artie waited to be the very last one. He was so nervous and Brittney was so distracted in trying to tell him to remain calm, they both forgot to close the clamp on his safety clip. Even worse, Brittney didn't connect the second one at all. Nobody noticed; they were too busy laughing while Brittney struggled helping Artie raise his hairy legs to get his ankles wrapped around the rope.

"You're doing good buddy, you're doing good," Heath yelled across to Artie.

"If you fall, you'll die," Spencer reminded Artie.

"Shut up, man," Artie screamed, looking like an overweight sloth, and moving about as slow as one.

"Oh no!" Brittney blurted. She was the first to see Artie's safety clip flopping below him. Heath saw right away why she gasped. The most observant of the boys saw it too, but nobody wanted to say anything. Then Spencer saw it.

"Artie!" Spencer blurted.

Heath ran over and put his hand around Spencer's mouth. "Shut up," Heath said sternly. "Don't say anything."

"Shut up, Spencer!" Artie shouted again, just about halfway across the obstacle.

"My arms are getting tired!" He groaned. "Can I just hang for a second?"

"No!" Brittney shrieked.

Artie kept letting his head rock back, trying to turn and see how much further he had to go. The back of his shirt, his armpits, and the seat of his pants were soaked in sweat.

"I need to take a break; my hands are burning!"

"Art. Do not let go!" Heath yelled as he started to hook his harness to the safety ropes, preparing for a rescue. Everyone heard the crack in Heath's nervous voice.

"But I'm slipping!"

"Art you're not strapped in!" Spencer blurted.

"What? What!" Artie stopped moving, he looked straight up at the sky, too tired to turn his head to the group. "What do you mean?"

"Just chill out, I am coming over to help, okay pal?" Heath said with an outstretched arm.

"My hands are burning, I'm gonna fall!"

"Arturo, don't let go!" Brittney pleaded.

"*Arturo*?" Ricky squashed his eyebrows together. "Artie's real name is Arturo?"

"You joking, man?" Dane asked. "Yo, Art! Ricky don't know your real name's Arturo!"

Artie's fat hands momentarily stopped their slipping, and he tried turning his head to the boys on the platform.

"Rick! You serious?" Artie huffed.

Ricky looked around; their chuckles confirmed he was the only one who didn't know Artie's real name.

"Well!" Rick called towards his struggling buddy, "Do you know my real name's Richard?"

Dez looked to Spencer and shook his head silently; this was news to him.

Artie tried blowing some hair and sweat out of his eyes, "Um, I have an uncle Ricky and his name is Ricardo. So I don't know; I guess we're eve—*Argh!* I'm slipping!"

"Art don't let go!" Brittney screamed.

The boys could only watch in terror as the rope dragged its way from Artie's palms, to his knuckles, to the very tip of his fingers.

And then Arturo lost his grip.

All the boys, Heath, and Brittney gasped at the same time. Artie's harness hardly had any slack in it, so when he let go, he only dropped about six inches before the lone safety line caught him. But the weight of Artie's body going fully limp, right in the middle of the line, caused the whole rope to oscillate. He swayed up and down with the cable.

"Art you need to get moving!" Brittney begged. She couldn't look away from his unclasped clip. The clamp held Artie as if he dangled from a single finger wrapped halfway around the line.

"My arms are too tired," Artie winced.

"Artie, you gonna slip off!" Great Dane warned.

Artie looked up and panicked. The way he churned his arms and legs made him look like a cat trying to get out of a swimming pool. The boys couldn't help but laugh.

Brittney reached her hands out as she spoke, looking across at Heath and the boys on the opposite platform. "He's going to break the clip. Heath, do something."

"Artie!" Heath roared. "Artie! Look at me. You need to stop moving around."

Artie froze and half turned his ear to his cabin leader.

"That clip is strong enough if you hold still. Do you understand? I'm coming over to get you but you have to hold still."

Artie tried to settle himself. Yet, he couldn't help but squirm as his nerves got to him. He kept bobbing his head up and down because his neck was sore from holding it upside down.

"Can you grab the crawl line?" Heath asked getting into position.

"I don't think so," Artie reached up, hardly getting his hands over his head.

"Alright, just don't move then. I'm coming."

"Don't die!" Dez yelled.

Heath had no trouble getting over to Artie, but once he got there, he froze. Heath looked around unsure of exactly what to do next. He tried to screw the clamp shut as step one, but it had bent too much and wouldn't close.

"Okay Art, I am going to lift you up, I need you to hold yourself up long enough for me to get your other safety strap hooked in. Okay?"

"I don't think I can lift myself up," Artie pouted.

"Then you're going to fall," Heath snapped, his face went red in an instant. "Lift up!"

None of the boys ever heard Heath talk to anyone like that before. His veins bulged out of the side of his neck, and his face went as red as his helmet; he looked pissed. Artie was so scared of the anger in Heath's voice, more scared than he was of falling, that he fully extended his hand to Heath. Heath pulled him up and hooked the dangling clip to the safety line, double-checking it was fully screwed shut.

"Okie dokie buddy," Heath said in a jolly voice, the redness gone from his face, and patting Artie's back with a smile. "You're all set over here, let's bring it in nice and slow, pal. Need help with your legs?"

Artie cracked half a smile, and nodded.

The Salamander boys cheered once Artie was secured to the line. When they got on the other side, Artie was greeted by high-fives from his friends. Everyone told Heath how awesome it was when he lifted Artie up while hanging upside down.

"Artie, I am so sorry," Brittney said while she spy-crawled her way across to meet up with the others, coming head first towards the boys.

"I forgive you," Artie said; he had to shake his head from staring so hard.

When she made it across, she peered into Artie's eyes; her own started to swell and water. "Artie, I am so sorry," she said again, and gave him a kiss on the cheek then placed her manicured hands on his shoulders. "We don't need to tell any of the camp rangers about this do we, buddy?"

He shook his head. Brittney smiled and hugged him tight. She held him so close that their stomachs touched. Every boy watched the exchange wishing they were the one who almost fell.

"Nobody died, that's what matters," Brittney winked. "Okay, time for the next obstacle."

CHAPTER 15

The First Stick

"Jiminy Crickets, look at this," Ranger Gladys said observing the front desk of the classroom. "What is this? Oh I'm going to have to speak with Camp Ranger Darlene about this."

Ranger Gladys was worked up over the gold plastic paint covering the front of the room. The desks, floor and even some chairs had splotches of the gold plastic drippings. She paced back and forth uncertain of what to pick up or clean first.

"Those fifth graders were in here making trophies, and they goobered up the whole front station," she said to no one in particular.

"Trophies?" Zach asked.

"Yes Mr. Taylor, the fifth graders made some trophies. Perhaps you'll notice the wooden stands along the side of the wall? Or the engraving tool? The plastic gold color paint that is seemingly on every surface of this classroom? Are you not very observant, Mr. Taylor?"

"I want a trophy," said big dumb Patrick Winkerton.

"How come we don't get trophies," Zach asked.

"Mr. Taylor, if you'd like to grace the fifth grade crafting class with your presence, I suggest you have that conversation with your parents," Ranger Gladys rubbed her eyebrows. All the girls laughed, and because they laughed, Zach thought he was cool.

"Alright, now everyone, let's pipe down," Ranger Gladys continued. "Today is an important day because we are going to learn how to string your lacrosse sticks. First, I want everyone to come up here—single file—and select your stick."

The students jumped out of their seats and hurried to the front of the room in one unorganized swarm.

"Single file. Single file campers, or we will all have to go back to our seats and we simply won't string lacrosse sticks at all."

Without their strung pockets, the lacrosse sticks looked more like hickory wood canes with the top handle curved in the shape of a question mark. All the sticks looked just about the same. After watching the video the day before, Ricky remembered how important the old sticks used to be to the original players. So, unlike Zach, Patrick, and Nolan, who grabbed the first one they got their hands on, Ricky inspected the sticks to find the perfect one for him. Whichever one he picked was going to be Ricky's first real lacrosse stick. He made sure to pick the best one. He couldn't help but smile with pride admiring it on the way back to his seat.

"You get the right one?" Claire teased. "Took you long enough."

Ricky inspected his stick again and felt the smoothness it had, and the strength of the finished hickory wood. He held it out with one hand and waived it a little to check its weight, and said, "Sure did."

"How are we going to know which stick is ours?" Paige asked from further up front sitting next to Danielle.

"Jumping Jupiter!" Ranger Gladys said clapping her hands together. "I'd forgotten with all the mess of this trophy nonsense up here. Thank you for reminding me."

Ranger Gladys huffed her way over to one of the cabinets in the front of the room and emerged with an armful of soldering irons. She told them to etch their names along the side of their sticks. When it was Ricky's turn to use the burner, instead of writing his name, he wrote *The First Stick*.

"What is that supposed to mean?" Claire asked.

"Well I never played lacrosse in my old town, so I wanted to write something cool to remember that this was my first stick ever. The one I use now is TJ's."

Ricky held out his stick proudly for Claire to see the inscription.

"Mr. Collins," Ranger Gladys grunted from over their shoulders.

"Yeah?" Ricky raised his eyebrows, doing his best to avoid looking guilty of something.

"You were instructed to write your name, nothing else," she said looking at the words.

"Should I erase it?" Ricky couldn't believe he had such insubordinate response, but Claire giggled. Ricky didn't know what it was, but he liked the cold rushing feeling that had just shot through his chest. He'd never talked back to a teacher like that.

"No, I suppose not," Ranger Gladys stepped back. "Very well, it seems appropriate enough." Then she addressed the rest of the room, "Students, you are instructed to write your names, and your names only, anything inappropriate will be confiscated."

"The first step in stringing a wooden stick," Ranger Gladys said with her example in hand for the class to see, "is adding the final wall to the head."

"Does anyone know what this is called?" Ranger Gladys displayed what looked like an eight-inch long miniature white picket fence made out of string.

Nobody knew what it was.

"This is what they call a gutwall."

"Ewww!" shouted many of the girls.

"Oh please campers," she scoffed. "We aren't using any real *guts*, that's just what it's called. The camp staff decided that the gutwall is a little too complicated to ask young campers to string themselves, so we've done that for you. Everyone come up here and get one."

"What is this made of?" Claire asked from her desk.

"Well, a truly traditional gutwall would have been made from buffalo rawhide," Gladys answered. "But ours are made out of nylon. We have a lot to do, class. Everyone hurry back to your seats."

Almost everyone needed Ranger Gladys to give a personalized demonstration as exactly how to string the nylon gutwall into their sticks. Claire was a natural. She knew managed to get the sidewall perfectly into place. Once strung correctly, the gutwall closed the gap in the question-mark shape of the stick's head. Claire helped Ricky feed the nylon strings into pre-drilled holes on his own stick. Then she helped him tie perfect knots to keep the wall firmly in place.

"Okay campers, listen here, listen here," Gladys exclaimed. "We've gone over our time for today. Those strings took a lot longer than I thought. Please bring your sticks up here, I'll keep them in the cabinet, and we'll pick up where we left off tomorrow. Let's hurry now!"

* * *

The next day in class, the students had to set up cardboard boxes over their desks, then put on a pair of rubber gloves. Ranger Gladys told the campers they needed to apply a coat of special wood finish on their gutwalls. Ricky wasn't sure what the name of the chemical was called, but Gladys made sure to have all the windows open and the ceiling fans spinning so that no one got sick from the fumes. As they waited for that to dry, the students tied the long vertical leather straps that would shape the pocket of their sticks. After that, they added the horizontal netting and shooting strings across the top of the pocket. The shooting strings reminded Ricky of the yellow laces used on construction boots.

"After these are done," Claire said focused on looping a knot through one of the thin leather straps in the pocket; "we're gonna have to test them out."

"Yeah, you want to play catch?" Ricky asked.

"Are you asking me out on a date or something?" Claire finally looked away from her stick and at Ricky.

Ricky could feel his face heating up like a stovetop, "No I just meant, like, I mean I thought, you said ... I just wanted to ... Catch."

"Take a breath, dude," she laughed and went back to stringing her stick. "I'm just joking around."

Ricky put his head down, and tried to focus on the over, under, loop-and-through instructions Gladys gave them about the lateral strings. "I know, I'm just kidding too," he lied.

"You are not," Claire poked him. "You're as red as a stop sign."

"Fine, then we don't have to play catch," he mumbled.

"Ricky, I want to. I'm just messing around, really. I want to play catch with you and our new sticks."

"Me too," he admitted.

"It's a play-date," she winked, causing another red wave to wash over his face.

CHAPTER 16

Outdoor Adventures

"Is this guy for real?"

The Salamanders often asked each other this question about their *Outdoor Adventures* class teacher, Camp Ranger Chester Steepdun. Since day one of the course, his strange antics both entertained and bewildered them. Steepdun wore the standard camp ranger khaki uniform and hiking boots, but instead of the normal drill sergeant hat and aviator sunglasses, he sported an olive colored fishing hat and cheap gas station sunglasses that sat on his sharp nose. Ranger Steepdun was older than Heath, but his permanently sunburnt leather skin made it hard to tell by how much. Most people struggled understanding anything he said because he spoke quickly in a high-pitched Australian accent.

"All right campers, time for the hike I told you about," Steepdun said in his squawky down-under voice. He said *campers*, but it sounded like *kempers*.

"We never talked about a hike," Spencer argued.

The first week of class Steepdun showed the Salamander boys a map of the campgrounds, and explained the boundaries and wildlife. He quizzed them about the different flora and fauna found in the area, but lost the answer key. He promised they'd take it again later. After the first week, Steepdun explained they'd get into the adventures part of the course.

Unlike the crafting class, the seventh and eighth graders had to be separated to keep track of everyone outside. The Salamanders checked into class at a supply garage in the northwest corner of the camp. A creek butted up to the brick structure, and beyond the creek stretched acres and acres of rocky forest terrain. Steepdun stood at the base of a bridge over the creek, waiving everyone along.

"Oh right, mate," Steepdun snapped his fingers at Spencer. "Alright then, okay so I forgot to tell you about the hike. Hope no one is wearing flip-flops." Without bothering to check anyone's shoes, Steepdun continued, "Good on ya. So we'll hike today, consider yourselves notified."

"How far?" TJ asked.

"Oh, I don't know, a few kilometers. Here; see what you've learned then," Steepdun pulled out a map and handed it to TJ. "Okay, so we're where we are, right? Good, someone show him. And we're going to go to about up here then, mates." He taped the map for a quick half-second with his thumb. "It's about that far. Alright let's go, lots to show along the way there too."

Ace looked at Dez, who looked at Spencer, who looked back at Ace; they all shook their heads. Nobody knew what the heck Steepdun was talking about.

"Stanton, you carry that map, there. Don't get us lost, okay chap?" he said to TJ.

"Do we need water?" Artie asked.

Steepdun snorted hard through his nostrils and turned around to look down at Artie, as if to admit Artie asked a good question. But Steepdun wasn't quite sure how to answer it. He removed his sunglasses with one hand and wiped them off with a red bandanna he pulled out of his shirt pocket with the other.

"Don't we need water?" Artie repeated with sweat already seeping through his t-shirt.

"Yeah man," Ace echoed, "could boil an egg out here."

Ranger Steepdun finally spit out whatever it was that he collected in his mouth after taking the long snort a few seconds ago; it flew about 10 yards across the bridge.

"Alright then, you two," he pointed at Dez and Great Dane. "Run in the garage, grab two packs, fill 'em with as many canteens as you can fit, and catch up. Stay on the blue markers, you'll find us."

"What if we get lost?" Dez speculated.

"Oh, just follow the blue markers, mate. You'll be fine; or Artie here will pass out knowing you two are blundering saps. Shove on then."

Ranger Steepdun started off over the bridge; the campers followed. They hiked deep into the forest, always making sure to stay on the blue trail. Steepdun often stopped to point out to the boys when he saw a warbler, a towhee, a pipit, and many other funny named birds that sounded even funnier when Steepdun tried to pronounce them in his accent. They jumped over dead logs, and hopped across from boulder to boulder. If any of their mothers were there, they'd be very upset with the risks that Steepdun permitted the campers to take, and he hardly ever looked back to watch.

"Whoa, here *kempers*," he said crouching under a large bush, or a very small tree. "Prunus emargintata."

"What the heck is that?" TJ shouted.

"This is a bitter cherry," he pulled off one of the small red bulbs from the bush.

"Can we eat it?" Artie asked.

"Not unless you want to get sick," Steepdun explained. "Come on mates, come over here and have a look at this thing."

"I can see it from here," answered TJ.

Steepdun held out one of the leaves to TJ, "Take a real gander at this here, really examine it, mate."

TJ took a minute to inspect the plant. He brought the leaf up close to his eyes and noticed how each vein ran along the stem and the way they offset so as not to be directly across from the other. TJ looked even closer and saw the tiny green shapes that looked to him like turtle shells. Each tiny shell, about half the size of a pinhead, were all unique. TJ wondered if these were the leaf's fingerprints.

"Now you see?" asked Steepdun.

"Yeah, pretty cool," TJ handed the leaf back to his camp ranger.

Finally, Dane and Dez came around the corner of the trail with the water bottles. Steepdun rolled the leaf up in his hands, then threw it to the ground and shouted, "Well there you are! We've been farting around here waiting for you two!"

"We couldn't find the packs," Dez explained, his flattop soaked in sweat.

"Okay, breaks over. We're going to head up to the next supply shed. That's where we'll learn to make fire."

The boys looked around and cheered. They felt like true wild men.

"Unless of course you're too tired, in which case, you can head back," Steepdun offered.

"If we go back, are you coming too?" Spencer caught on to the subtly of Steepdun's offer.

"No, I left me knife up there yesterday; got to go get it. All right then, so we're done with the water, aren't we? Come on *kempers*, hop to."

Eventually, they rounded the bend on the trail, and the path opened up to a clearing. The flat red rocks swallowed up most of the ground. About the distance of two football fields from where the path widened, they could see the shed that Steepdun mentioned, some benches, and a small dirt bike chained up to the side of the shed.

"This thing always gets a little jammed," Steepdun said after entering the combination on the padlock of the shed. "It's the humidity; it sticks the door. Sometimes you gotta pry it open." As he spoke, Steepdun reached into his front pocket and pulled out a tactical pocketknife and wedged it into the door lock.

"What the heck is that, man?" Spencer said pointing to the knife with four outstretched fingers.

"Thought you lost the knife?" Dane reminded him.

"Did I?" Steepdun scratched his head inspecting the knife. "Well, I guess I found it then, didn't I? Alright *kempers* well, let's take a break here, then we'll head back."

"You gotta be kiddin' me," Ace threw up his arms and dropped to one of the nearby benches. "We came all the way out here for nothing!"

Ranger Steepdun went into the shed and tinkered around while he continued his conversation with whoever was within an earshot. The boys spread themselves out around the picnic area, and could hear him banging stuff around, while he searched for whatever it was he was looking for. The rattling sounds of untangling metal fencing, crashes from falling buckets and tools, and the frustrated bangs of moving large items weren't enough to keep Steepdun from talking through his unorganization.

"I wouldn't say that it was for nothing. Have you ever been here before?" Steepdun asked.

"No, none of us have," said Marcus. "You knew that."

"Well now you have, and you'll have to come back here to get to the over night, anyways."

"The what?" Ben Li asked fanning himself down with his golf visor.

The rummaging sounds from inside the shed temporarily stopped, "I didn't tell you about the over night?"

"No!" Spencer's blond hair lay flat and wet over his eyebrows from the sweat; he was hot and agitated.

"I'll have to do that then, okay. *Eureka*! Here they are!"

Steepdun emerged from the shed with two old splintered shovels.

"Tell us about what?" Ben asked.

Steepdun took a swig of water out of a canteen he apparently had in his backpack the whole time. "The over night," he explained. "I coulda sworn I mentioned it. You all, and your *kaben* leader? We're to trek out here to the next checkpoint and spend the night outside."

Each boy expressed his excitement differently. Most of them smiled, others cheered looking around to share high-fives. Almost all of them had commentary.

"Where are we going to sleep?"

"You never told us that!"

"What will we eat?"

"How do we get there?"

"When is it?"

"What about wolves?"

"How come Heath didn't tell us?"

"Seriously, what will we eat?"

Ranger Steepdun raised both hands to signal to the campers to quiet down. "We'll set up *kemp*, cook our meals, and sleep out under the night sky."

"What will we eat for dinner?" Artie asked a third time.

"I'm no chef, but we'll cook somethin' over the *kemp*fire," Steepdun said with his palms raised to his side. "First, we'll need to learn to make a fire, so let's get in the shed here and look for some shovels."

TJ lifted his chin up to the sky, and groaned, "They're right there!"

"Oh good on you, mate. That's right."

Steepdun had some boys help dig a pit for the fire, while others searched for rocks to line the pit with, and the rest were told to forage for dry leaves, twigs, and branches. Steepdun demonstrated how to build a tinder tepee. They started with the smallest driest leaves at the bottom, then wrapped twigs around the outside of the dry pile. Finally, they stacked larger branches and sticks around the smaller ones in the shape of a tepee.

"Are you going to teach us how to make fire with rocks and flint?" Marcus asked.

"What? Rocks, and flint? No mate, I was going to use this here,'" Steepdun pulled a lighter out of his pocket. It was like any common lighter the boys had seen a hundred times at the check-out counters of grocery stores and gas stations.

"That's cheating," accused Spencer.

"Mates, if you know you're going *kempin'*, and you know you're goin' to be buildin' a fire, then I say come prepared."

"A real outdoorsman makes fire with sticks," Great Dane grunted.

The rest of the boys responded in agreement. They wanted to learn how to make fire with sticks. Steepdun took a moment thinking how he'd handle the situation then checked his watch.

"I'll do a tutorial."

"Step one: you get your tinder," Steepdun motioned to the pile of dry leaves the campers collected. "Step two: you get the driest branch you can find, and you cut off its bark. Then slice out a piece about a foot long. It has to be from the same branch," Steepdun said cutting the two pieces and showing how the smaller piece fit like a puzzle into the first piece.

"Step three: you need to shave the tip of the small piece at a sharp angle, so it has a flat edge. Then you rub it against the wood on the side you shaved the bark off."

Steepdun rubbed the stick back and fourth against the wood so quickly that his arms looked like he was holding on to a jackhammer.

"When it starts smoking, press harder and push faster. When this black ash starts smoking real good and long, like so, you bring the tinder to the ashes, and put it into the tinder nest like this here. Be real careful. And you blow on it."

Steepdun stood up holding the ball of dry leaves and grass in his open hands and carefully blew on it, as he made his way a little closer to the fire pit. The white smoke grew thicker around his hands and he blew a little harder. The orange embers pulsed brightly. Then in a flash, the bright embers turned to small flames. The boys watched in total silence and followed their camp ranger over to the fire pit. The entire ball of tinder lit in Steepdun's hands and he dropped it carefully over the tepee of twigs in the fire pit.

"You probably still need to blow on it for a bit till the flames really pick up."

"That was awesome!" Spencer shouted.

"I've never seen anyone do that before!" TJ exclaimed.

"How'd you learn that?" asked Ace.

"Well, like I just showed you mates, its about as simple as that. And I'll tell ya' all again, if you're going *kempin'* you'd be better off with a box of matches or a lighter than trying to fuss with all that mess here. It's a waste of time, really."

Steepdun's watch beeped. "Oh goodness, speaking of time we gotta get the heck out of here. Use them shovels here to bury the fire, quickly mates it's the safest way. Hurry up with all that; we're late for lunch."

CHAPTER 17

Why It's Called 'Lax'

Ricky felt every set of eyes in the Grand Hall follow him while he walked to his table, alone. The Salamanders' outdoor class took much longer than usual, so Ricky had no one to sit with during lunch. A camp ranger with his clipboard rubbernecked his way over to Ricky to investigate.

"Where are your friends young man?" the camp ranger's lips hardly moved under his mustache.

"I don't know, sometimes their outdoor class takes long."

"Ah, that figures with Ranger Steepdun, but why aren't you in class?"

"I'm in the crafts class," Ricky said looking down at his food, embarrassed, but also proud to be holding his new wooden stick.

"Crafts class, ay? Why didn't you take Outdoor Adventures?"

Ricky rolled his eyes, and sunk deep into his chair while he signed. As he opened his mouth to explain for the hundredth time that his parents insisted he take the crafting class to be a more well-rounded citizen, Claire Minnich sat down across from him. The camp ranger cleared his throat, nodded to Claire, and walked away.

"Anyone sitting here?" she teased.

"I guess not," Ricky could feel the hot coals of embarrassment on his face.

"I've heard about people eating lunch in the cafeteria at school alone, but never at summer camp," she went on.

"They've never taken this long to come back from class before."

"Well that's good, then we can play catch. Hurry up and eat."

Zach Taylor, Nolan, and Patrick with lunch trays in hand, circled around Ricky and Claire.

"Hey look at this guys," said Zach. "This must be the couples only section."

Both Nolan and Patrick laughed; Ricky raised his eyebrows wondering how that comment was funny at all.

"This must be the loser section," said Patrick.

Nolan snickered at Patrick's remark, but Zach scrunched his face and tilted his head back in disapproval that Patrick tried making the same joke with only a slight modification.

"Are you coming to join?" Ricky tried to fire back, but not quite loud enough to be assertive.

Claire kept her lips tight together and gave Ricky a look that asked him to keep quiet and let them walk away.

"Shut up butt wipe," Zach looked back for laughs, and got them. "How'd your loser trophy turn out?"

"Don't you have any other seventh grade girls to try to impress?" asked Claire as she whipped her hair around like a lion's mane.

"Whoa sassy," Nolan said raising his palms.

"Enjoy your lunch, love losers," Zach tapped his wooden stick on the edge of the table. Then, tapping Ricky's stick, Zach said, "Be careful with that thing." He grimaced, making sure to make eye contact with both of them, "Wouldn't want to lose that, loser."

The tree of three of them chuckled together and walked away.

"I hate those guys," Ricky said once they were out of hearing distance.

"Don't let them bother you," Claire advised. "If they see that they've gotten under your skin they'll bother you all next year at school."

"Of course they only come over here when all the other guys are gone," Ricky observed.

"Are you done?" Claire asked. "Let's go play catch."

* * *

All the practice in the world wouldn't have helped Ricky from being nervous while playing with Claire. She was a natural. Claire could catch, cradle, switch hands, and throw the ball back to Ricky in one motion as nimble as a ballerina. Ricky fumbled with his new stick. He snatched at the ball a few times, causing it to bounce off the sidewall, and then he'd have to go chase after it. Throwing it over Claire's head was also a risk, so he kept throwing it low, too low. He accidentally one-hopped it to her more than a few times. Ricky used the new stick as an excuse for his bad throws. He tried to point out how in a real game he'd never use a wooden stick. But Claire pointed out her stick was new to her too, yet she wasn't having any trouble.

"What the crap Ricky?" Claire shouted after the ball bounced again several feet in front her legs, and rolled away. "Do you know why people call lacrosse, *lax*?" She answered her own question before he had a chance to respond, "Because you have to be *relaxed* to play it!"

"I know, sorry," he said, feeling the embarrassed rush from his chest to the top of his hair follicles.

"You have to learn how to not be so tense."

"I don't want to throw it over your head," he confessed.

"Just do it!" Her blonde curly hair covered her face tangling in the wind. "Throw it high over my head one time just to get it over with."

She whipped the ball at him, straight into the pocket of his stick.

She's right, he said to himself. He took a deep breath, then threw it high and fast over Claire's head. She had to go chase after it.

"Finally," she yelled retrieving the ball. "Now it's out of your system. Do you feel better?"

"I kinda do," he smiled. "That really worked."

Ricky didn't drop a catch or miss another ball after that. Whether he threw right or left-handed didn't matter, his passes landed directly on target. Claire even admitted that for only learning how to play a few weeks ago, Ricky was getting good.

CHAPTER 18

The Commissioner's Office

The boys returned from their hike shouting and whistling at Ricky and Claire from pretty far off. She decided to go back to her friends before they got too close. Ricky stood in the middle of Cooke Field waiting for the Salamander cabin crew to see his new stick.

"Where have you been?" he asked.

"Ranger Steepdun is a lunatic," Spencer answered.

"Yeah but it was awesome," Dez added, drenched in sweat.

"Is this the arts and crafts stick?" asked TJ.

"Whoa," said everyone else.

"We're out makin' fires, meanwhile Craftsman over here gettin' a new stick an' fallin' in love with Claire Minnich," Ace mocked.

"When are you two going to get married?" Artie asked crossing his hands over his heart.

"Maybe he's still in love with Hannah," Ben Li said as sincere as he always was, and as usual, unclear whether he was tying to be insulting.

"Will you guys shut up?" Ricky waived them off, hardly able to contain his smile. "Seriously where have you been?" He asked again trying to change the subject.

While the boys passed around Ricky's stick, and admired the job well done with stringing the pocket, they told him about the overnight.

"Do I get to come? Even if I'm not in the class?" Ricky worried.

"You'll probably be sleeping in the Camp Commissioner's Office," TJ laughed.

"I'm going with, I better!" Ricky said, and snatched his stick back from out of the hands of whoever had it. "I'm going to talk to Heath right now."

"I'll come with you," TJ jogged after him. "Did Claire say anything about Danielle saying anything about me?"

* * *

Ricky and TJ barraged into the fourth grade girls' high ropes course session to confront Heath. The fourth grade version of the obstacle course was hardly anything exciting at all, and Ricky demanded that Heath talk to him about the overnight. He stood under the platform yelling up to Heath.

"Ricky, I'm a little busy right now," Heath said while a young girl tried to make her way across a balance beam, Brittney cheered her on from the other end.

"All the guys are getting to go on an overnight in the woods, and they said you're going too, but what am I going to do?" Ricky blurted.

"Is that your stick from class?" Heath asked temporarily losing his focus.

"Heath!" Brittney crossed her arms.

"I'll look at it later. And I don't know Ricky, you'll probably get to come with."

"Do you promise I'll go?" Ricky begged.

"Before dinner, you and I will go down to the Camp Commissioner's Office and sort it out."

"Hi Brittney," TJ said bobbing his head.

"Hi?" Brittney answered raising her eyebrows.

"How's Danielle doing?"

"Will you two please get out of here?" Brittney demanded.

"Okay for real, you guys got to go. Ricky, we'll talk to Commissioner Powell; it'll be fine."

"Tell Danielle I said hi," TJ winked at Brittney.

"Bye!" Brittney didn't waive.

* * *

Heath led the way while he and Ricky walked down the rustic halls of the Camp Commissioner's Office. Before they turned the corner towards the receptionist's desk, they could both hear her chomping her gum from down the hall. The receptionist sat at her desk, with freshly painted mint green fingernails, typing about 200 words per minute.

"Hey there, Heath," the receptionist spoke somehow without ever closing her lips.

"Hi Margaret, is the boss in?"

"Oh and look at you," Margaret said to Ricky. "You never called."

Heath and Ricky exchanged glances; Ricky assured his cabin leader he didn't know what she was talking about.

"Yeah, the Boss is in. I'll tell him you're here. Take a seat."

Margaret picked up the phone and spoke into it, "Commissioner Powell ... Yes ... Mr. Heath McPhair is here to see you ... he's a cabin leader ... he's with a camper ... no visible injuries ..." she covered the phone with her hand and ran her eyes over Ricky and Heath, then spoke back into the phone. "I don't think so, sir." She covered up the phone again and asked, "Is it an emergency?"

Heath said no, Ricky said yes.

Margaret took a stern look at Heath, then back at Ricky and winked at him, she spoke back into the phone, "Yes sir it's an emergency ... I understand."

She slammed the phone down and swiveled in her chair towards a back cabinet, grabbing a clipboard. Then she rolled her chair back over and almost slamming into her desk, held the clipboard out in front of her towards the two waiting.

"Please sign in, it'll be just a few minutes."

When Ricky stood up and reached for the clipboard, she dropped it just before Ricky was close enough to catch it.

"Too slow," Margaret chomped on her gum as the clipboard fell off the edge of the desk. She swiveled back in her chair to face the computer and started typing furiously again.

"What's with her?" Ricky leaned over whispering to Heath.

"She's just messing around," Heath explained. "Margaret's the best. So is this your stick?" Heath took the wooden stick from Ricky.

"This is pretty well done," he observed feeling the weight in his hand and bobbing it up and down to check its balance. "Did you carve this?"

"No, we just did the engravings, but I strung the pocket myself."

"The first stick," Heath read the engraving aloud. "This is wicked cool man, I'm going to have to talk to Ranger Gladys and see if I can get one somehow. I bet the guys were jealous."

"Thanks. Yeah, everyone thought it was neat."

"Are either of you thirsty or anything?" Margaret asked.

"Can I have a glass of water?" Heath answered.

Margaret just kept on typing away without acknowledging the request. Then she glanced up at Ricky, "Have you ever met Commissioner Powell?"

Ricky shook his head.

"He's the head overseer of the whole camp, I hope you aren't in any trouble. He'll send you home," Margaret explained. The next thing she said, she did it trying to imitate a Southern man's voice:

"Too many campers in this here park, we gotta send 'em home. They git hurt? Send 'em home. They actin' up? Send 'em home. Vandalism? Send—" Margaret cut herself off to slam down on the phone right at the exact instant it started to ring and with one hand she popped it off the base and caught it in mid-air. "Yes, sir?"

Margaret banged the phone down, and pointed for them to go into the office.

The walls in Commissioner Powell's had nothing hanging on them. Apart from a mountain lion rug, the only thing in the office was the desk, a couch facing the desk, and a file cabinet on the sidewall; there were no pictures. The lights weren't turned off completely, but they may as well have been, Commissioner Powell kept them at a low dim. The room's single window was directly behind the desk, with the blinds shut almost completely, the sunlight revealed only Powell's silhouette to anyone who entered. He sat straight as a statute in a billow of smoke from his old cherry wood pipe. The smoke spilled over around the brim of his cowboy hat.

"Well?" he asked in a deep voice that sounded as if it belonged to an old, weathered Louisiana bullfrog.

Heath assured Ricky it was safe to walk in, and the two approached the hazy figure. Heath sat down casually and crossed a foot over his thigh. When Ricky sat down on the sofa, he sunk deep, all the way to the bottom of the cushion. Despite the darkness in the room, Commissioner Powell kept his sunglasses on. His thick grey goatee, like wolf's fur, covered his rounded chin and neck.

"Afternoon, there Heath," Commissioner Powell said. "And you're Ricky Collins, right?"

"Yes, sir," Ricky tried to sit up from the quicksand couch while he spoke. Ricky's mouth was dry; he wished he asked Margaret for water, but doubted she would have given it to him.

"Ha!" Commissioner Powell slammed his hand on his desk, shaking the unlit lamp and rattling his coffee mug.

"Boy, I knew it! I always pride m'self on knowing the campers."

He slapped his hands and rubbed them together, then rocked back and forth in his Adirondack rocking chair. Ricky had no idea what it was like to be in the principal's office, but he doubted any principal's sat behind their desks in rocking chairs.

"What can I do you for?" Commissioner Powell asked.

Heath answered for Ricky, "Well, Mister—uh Commissioner Powell, Sir. We have a small problem regarding the Outdoor Adventures class."

"Steepdun didn't try 'n shoot an apple off your head with a bow 'n arrow did he?"

"What?" Heath turned to Ricky. "No Sir. There was none of that."

"Ah, thank goodness," Powell stroked his goatee. "For the record on that, nobody ever got hurt, he's a great shot. Still, parents don't like the idea of someone aiming arrows at their children. Any-who, out with it then, what's going on? What's the trouble with the great outdoors, young man?"

Heath shook his head and waived his hands at the commissioner, "No, the problem is that Ricky isn't in the outdoors class."

"Not in the outdoor adventure class?" Powell focused his shielded stare on Ricky. "This is your first year at camp, isn't it?"

"Yes, sir."

"I suppose your mommy and daddy thought coming to Camp Tallawanda would be adventuresome enough for you, didn't they? Wouldn't let you take the adventure class wouldn't they?"

Heath spoke for Ricky, "Yes sir. Hit the nail right on the head."

"Ha!" Powell clapped his hands once then pounded his right hand on the desk again. "Been doin' this a long time son, ain't nothin' I haven't seen least once before. Well alright, so you got stuck in the crafts class—which is mighty educational—is that the lacrosse stick you made in there?"

"Yes sir," Ricky handed it over for the commissioner to take a look at it.

Commissioner Powell measured the stick's weight in his hand the same way Heath did just a few minutes earlier.

"This is really well done. You know we carved these all here on site? We cut from our hickory trees; we steamed and dried them over the fall and winter. It takes almost six months to dry these out, you know? A lot of care went into making this thing. You did a nice job with the gutwall here, and the pocket looks about right. Little crooked on the engraving but that's aesthetic," Powell observed giving the stick back to Ricky.

"Thanks, I really like it. I liked learning about how they—"

"—But a young boy like you wants to be out doing the adventures and the hiking, and the learning to tie knots, and building fires, and all the rest, am I right?"

"Well, sir," Heath tried to get a full sentence out of his mouth without interruption. "The class overnight is coming up. Ricky's the only one who isn't in the class, and—"

"—And he wants to go with?" Powell motioned with his hands for Heath to get on with it, as if Heath had been telling a long story. Ricky nodded in agreement.

"Easy. We'll call your parents, get their permission, it's no problem at all."

"They'll say no," Ricky blurted out.

Commissioner Powell stroked his goatee, and rocked slowly, "I see. So you're proposing that we circumnavigate the required parental consent procedures and permit you to have the adventure?"

Ricky nodded, pretty sure he understood the commissioner's question, "They won't let me go."

Commissioner Powell methodically filled up his cherry wood pipe. His old grey hands carefully packed its contents to the brim. He reached over and opened a small pine box from the edge of his desk to pull out a redheaded match. He lit the match with his thumbnail, and held the pipe with the other hand to his goatee-covered mouth. He puffed slowly and the smoke soon covered his face, and rolled around the brim of his hat. He rocked backwards for another minute, and then took his sunglasses off to polish them while the pipe hung from his mouth. Commissioner Powell had bright blue eyes tucked behind his wrinkled face. Powell made eye contact with each of them, then hid behind his sunglasses once again. He took the pipe out of his mouth before he spoke.

"And what if something happens to you? What if you get dragged off by a bear into the woods and get eaten alive? What am I supposed to tell your mother?"

"Has that ever happened?" Ricky gulped. He could feel the color leaving his face.

"Ha!" Powell slammed the table again. "Boy are you out of your mind? You'd be eaten by a pack of wolves sooner than a bear. Of course you can go!"

"Really?" Ricky stood up from the couch.

Powell waived his hand like he was swatting an imaginary fly from his face, "You're a young boy, you need adventure, you're mommy don't need to know 'bout everything, now does she?"

"No she doesn't," Ricky shook his head. "Thank you, thank you, Sir."

"Of course; if you do get eaten out there, I'll have to deny this conversation occurred."

Ricky laughed for the first time since walking into the office. "Yes, yes, thank you, Mr. Commissioner, sir."

"That's all, then. Good day," and he pointed them to the door with his pipe.

When they walked out of the office Margaret was at her desk reading an old newspaper with her feet crossed resting near the phone. She wasn't wearing shoes, but she had on thick wool hiking socks. She peaked over the top of the paper just to confirm it was only the two of them walking out of the office, then her head popped back down out of sight.

"Heath, you come back anytime for that glass of water now," her mint green fingernails waived goodbye over the newspaper.

CHAPTER 19

The Overnight

The boys in Salamander cabin bounced off the walls packing their bags and double-checking their gear for a night in the woods. Already away at summer camp, the trip counted to them as a sleepover within the vacation. They buried Heath in questions.

"Are we going to need a tent?"

"Is it going to be cold?"

"What are we going to eat?"

"How long is the hike?"

"Can I bring a flashlight?"

"Have you ever been there before?"

"Why can't someone tell me what we're going to eat?"

Heath stood up in the middle of the cabin and blew his coaching whistle.

Whhsssshhhppp!

"Guys," Heath barked, and the room momentarily fell silent. "Shut. Up."

Heath picked up his backpack for everyone to see. "This is about being in the woods, like a real adventure. You don't need anything. We're going for one night, and we'll be back in the morning. The less you pack, the better the adventure. All I have in my backpack is my sweatpants, a sweatshirt, a bottle of water, my pocket knife, and a flashlight."

"What 'bout a toothbrush?" asked Ace.

"No toothbrush," Heath smiled.

Somebody pounded on their cabin door; Dez dropped his bag to answer it. As soon as Dez cracked the door just a bit, Ranger Steepdun let himself into the cabin. He wore the same khaki park ranger outfit as always, but substituted his normal pack for a much larger blue and green one with buckled straps around his waist. Artie hoped he needed the bigger bag to bring food. "Alright, *kempers*; hello Heath. Are we about ready?"

"What are we going to eat?" asked Artie.

"I brought some provisions, don't worry, mate. Now then, who's the new guy?" he pointed at Ricky with his thumb.

"I'm Ricky Collins."

"Alright, hello there, I'm Ranger Chester Steepdun; introduction complete. Good on ya for comin' along, mate."

"Alright Steepdun, guys, are we ready?" Heath clapped his hands together once.

"I'd say we're ready to shove off then Heath," Steepdun answered. "Best to go now and avoid making the whole trek in the dark if we can avoid it."

* * *

Steepdun and Heath lead the way to the campsite. Ranger Steepdun instructed Great Dane to be the caboose. Steepdun said in a large group it was important to have a designated watchdog. He told Dane not to allow anyone behind him at any time, and to take the responsibility very seriously, so no one got lost. Ricky walked in the middle of the pack with Ace and TJ. Unlike the rest of the cabin, Ricky hadn't been so deep into the woods yet that summer, all the trees, and large red rocks, and fallen logs fascinated him.

When they left for the hike, the sun had just started to slip behind the mountains, turning the sky purple. The trees stopped casting shadows and the green in the leaves lost its afternoon pop. The sound of birds and insects filled the air, along with the camper's trampling over fallen branches and whirling insults at each other.

"Have a look here," Steepdun said pointing at a small bird with rust colored shoulders and yellow stripes on its head and underbelly. "Which one of you likes all the dirty jokes? Spencer, want to tell the new guy what that one is there?"

Spencer smiled ear to ear and jiggled his eyebrows, "That's a dickcissel."

Ricky laughed with all the others.

"Good on you, mate. Okay, let's keep it moving," Steepdun planted on his walking stick and turned back up towards the trail.

"What other stuff does that guy teach you?" Ricky asked the guys on either side of him.

"See that branch hangin' from that tree up there?" Ace pointed up to a tree a few yards into the woods off to their right-hand side. He pointed out the thick branch that had been broken off but dangled stuck from the tree's other branches. Ricky acknowledged that he saw it.

"That's called a widow-maker," Ace explained. "Steepdun says you never make a tent under a hangin' branch, cause it could fall on ya. We learn 'bout that kinda stuff."

"I wish I could be in that class," said Ricky.

"No you don't," said Dez from in front of them. He spoke without looking backwards. "You like being the Craftsman and spending your time with Claire."

"And you get to keep a very nice souvenir." Ben added. "I wish I could have a wooden lacrosse stick like yours."

"Seriously," said TJ. "If I knew they'd be giving those things out, I woulda signed up too."

The troop continued on into the woods for another full hour. Steepdun insisted that they stopped at the maintenance garage before they took a break. Once they made it to the garage, he admitted they needed to stop there for a few supplies he forgot to get that morning.

"It's not too far from here," Steepdun promised. "We'll take a ten minute break or so, then shove off."

Beyond the garage checkpoint, they had to walk through a large prairie clearing. The grass was tall, and the trail was hardly more than six inches wide at some points as it bottlenecked through the high wheat colored grass.

"Don't go into the long grass," Dez joked in a strange accent, referencing one of everyone's favorite movies.

By the time the boys crossed the grassy field to get back into the woods, it was nearly dark. The boys who brought them, all turned on their flashlights. The far off hoots from owls replaced the chirping birds, and a cold dark blanket pulled over the forest canopy tapped in for the setting sun. The flashlights made it easy enough to see in the direction they were walking, but looking out to either side, there was nothing but darkness.

"Are there any wolves out here?" asked Ben Li.

"With as loud as we're all being out here, I doubt they'd come any close to us, mate," Steepdun almost shouted it as he was unsure how far back the furthest guy was walking. "Oh, I forget, we need to do a head count here, so as not to forget anyone. Probably should have done a count after that garage there."

After going over the next hill, the ground leveled out, and the trees cleared away again to reveal a large wooden tower. The open field allowed for the light from the moon and stars to fill the cloudless night. Everything was lit under the pale cool light of the moon. They could see almost perfectly, except the world seemed painted black and white from the moonlight. The tower was shaped like a 20-foot tall outdoor deck. Its round smooth columns were about as thick as a telephone pole. Permanent ladders, built into the legs of the tower, stood on both ends of the long side of the structure.

Steepdun told the Salamanders to put their bags up on the deck and claim their spots for the night.

"*Kempers* climb up there, and claim you spots for the night," Steepdun pointed. "And hurry up. We'll need to get on to building our fire."

The top of the platform wasn't much more than a flat outdoor patio. A large mat, and several smaller mats were sprawled out across so that it wouldn't be too unbearably hard to sleep on. There was also a stack of sleeping bags for the boys to use. Steepdun promised they washed the sleeping bags regularly, but Ricky imagined his mother wouldn't think so. Wooden banisters lined the platform on all sides, and little glow lights signaled where the ladders opened. There was no real danger of anyone falling off. What the boy's didn't expect to see was there was no roof. The platform sat uncovered like a backyard deck.

"Look at all the stars up here, y'all" Ace noticed.

"We're literally sleeping outside, no tent?" Marcus asked down to Steepdun. Both Ace and Marcus spoke in their nighttime voices, which is to say that they neither whispered, nor yelled, but spoke in loud hushes.

Steepdun spoke in a normal outside voice, "Of course we're sleeping under the stars, I told you that didn't I? I meant to anyways."

"Come on down guys," Heath waived. "Let's get this fire going."

"Are we gonna get s'mores?" Artie asked. "I snagged some s'mores supplies from the cafeteria just in case." Artie hobbled his way down the ladder as Marcus stood over him shining a light on the ground below. The boys exited from both sides, and the second to last guy down held the flashlight, so the last one could see where to step on the ladder.

"Make sure you all go pee before you get to bed, too." Heath said. "That's a long ladder to have to climb down at night.

"I'm gonna piss off the ledge," Great Dane bragged.

"You'll probably pee the bed," TJ joked.

Ranger Steepdun brought a small shovel—the kind Ricky had seen soldiers carry on their backs in old war movies—and dug a fire pit with it. The boys begged Steepdun to start the fire with twigs again. Steepdun went on to lecture them about the importance of being prepared, and that a proper outdoorsman would be prepared and bring a lighter. However, after giving his speech about preparation, Steepdun admitted he couldn't find his lighter. Heath however, was prepared; he had a box of matches in his pack.

Steepdun pointed at Heath, "There *kempers*, ya see? Always be prepared: fail to plan, plan to fail. That's what I say."

"All you brought to eat was beans and popcorn?" Artie complained. "Good thing I brought s'mores."

"What's wrong with beans and popcorn, mate?" asked Ranger Steepdun. "We're on an adventure, sleeping out in the open sky, what did ya expect? Lasagna?"

Steepdun heated the refried beans over the fire while the campers ran around exploring their new area. The forest path wound sideways and vertically, up the mountainside. They knew they'd been walking for a while, but when they looked out from the tower and saw Camp Tallawanda's cabin lights flickering through tree line, they realized just how far into the trail they'd gone.

CHAPTER 20

"Shoulda seen your face!"

"Tell us a scary story?" Ben Li requested over the crackling fire.

The Salamander boys sat in a circle on logs and stumps around the bonfire. They'd each found the perfect stick for roasting marshmallows, and used pocketknives to carve the tips into sharp prongs. The stars sparkled through the depths of the deep blues and black night sky. A cloud of uneasiness fell around the boys after Ben's suggestion. The darkness that leaned against each of the campers' backs reminded them how far away hiked from their familiar campgrounds. Ben's question snapped the group out of a temporary trance caused from staring at the mesmerizing dance of the flames.

"Oh, I don't know," Heath said, poking at a marshmallow he dropped in the bonfire. "I'm not really sure I know any. What about you, Steeps?"

Steepdun widened his eyes as he stared straight into the flames, his sharp nose glowing red against the blaze, "I only tell but the one story," he said without looking away. "The only true scary story I know." The fire retreated from Steepdun's words and huddled itself lower on the logs.

Who would be the bravest one to ask to hear it, they wondered.

"Tell us," Marcus demanded.

Steepdun said shifting his weight in his seat, deciding if he should tell the story. He cleared his throat; spit into the fire and said, "Well I guess you're all old enough."

Ricky looked around to make sure he wasn't the only one suddenly feeling uncomfortable; he wasn't. Ricky watched as Spencer's entire body shuddered at the uneasy vibes coming from Steepdun's direction. Heath leaned over into the fire and when he came back to a seated position made sure to scooch a few inches away from the camp ranger.

"I came by the story from a chap with the name of Olzfeld. He don't work here no more. But one day, bout maybe four or five years back, him and I were out on dirt bikes out here, fixing the boundary fences. Probably 'bout another hour hike from where we are now. We ended up staying out too late, woulda been too dangerous to ride the bikes back in the dark. So, we made camp for the night. Anyway, we make a fire, and this Olzfeld guy starts tellin' me this story.

"And he's bit of an ugly guy mind you. Nasty scar he had round the back of his neck. Legend has it, he says: Back in 1928—this Olzfeld tells me—there was a small town 'bout 40 kilometers east of camp, off the road. These two guys robbed a bank. During the heist, the U.S. Marshalls chased 'em out of the bank, and they tried getting away on horses. They rode their horses out into the woods. The coppers started shootin' at 'em, and both their horses were killed, poor brutes. So, the robbers, carrying only one sack o' money each that they could handle, make off deeper into the bush. These were real clever mates, Olzfeld tells me—and his scar is looking even more gruesome in the firelight—and they were able to outrun the cops. Well, luck would have it, that they somehow meander their way onto the camp's property, and this was while the camp was in session mind you, this Olzfeld guy says to me."

Steepdun adjusted himself on his log, and spat into the fire before continuing again. "Apparently, what these two bank robbers did, is they came through the outer edge of the camp, thinking it was an old military training base or something. Fearin' they'd have to make a run for it, they bury the money. Then, they tried to sneak around the outer boarders of the camp. They come across a class of kids out on a hike, just as we are now. The thieves take two young *kempers* hostage. When the police arrived, the whole thing ended in a shootout. Neither the bank robbers nor the *kempers* survived. Poor kids. Eventually, the police found the money but this Olzfeld guy told me, the ghosts of the kids can be heard running through the woods, trying to escape from the bandits. But they can only run as far away as where the shootout happened, trapped forever," Steepdun said all this without blinking.

There was a pause for a moment as the boys let the story sink in, some looking to Heath throughout the tale to try and determine if it was true.

"That's not even the scary part," Steepdun continued just before anyone spoke out. "I had nightmares the same night this Olzfeld guy told me the story. I coulda sworn the ghosts of those *kempers* came to visit me. I wake up in the middle of the night, and I'm alone. No Olzfeld, no second dirt bike, nothing, just me. When they came to find me in the morning, everyone at the camp said it was just me who went out the day before. They thought I was crazy about thinking anything about this Olzfeld guy, nobody said they'd even heard of him. And I asked them all about the bank robbery story, and nobody ever heard of it."

After Steepdun shared this last bit of information, even Heath shifted in his seat, not sure what to make of it. He looked at Steepdun with an open mouth. Any boy who wasn't nervous yet, lost his courage after looking at Heath.

"Bullcrap!" Spencer's voice cracked. "You're full of it, that ain't true. And no one ever told me anything about any kind of robbers at this camp."

"Yeah, no way!" Great Dane said from across the fire. "My parents grew up coming to this camp, and never told me about a bank robbery or anything like that. Never."

"Well that's what I thought," Steepdun agreed "Then this guy goes and disappeared on me. Everyone thought I'd lost my marbles."

They didn't answer.

"And you know what else?" Steepdun whispered. "I think I was brainwashed."

No one spoke. The sky felt darker, and only the crickets and the crackling of the fire cut the silence. Everyone seemed to move a little closer to his neighbor, and a little further from Steepdun. The boys looked to each other for reassurance, not knowing what to believe. Heath was no help, as he too gazed at Steepdun with doubt and the courage gone from his face.

"I've got the scar," Steepdun whispered quietly. He leaned over towards Heath who was sitting closest to him, and Steepdun reached his hand to the back of his neck to show Heath the scar. Heath bent over to take a closer look when Steepdun turned around quickly and grabbed him with both hands.

"Gotcha!" Steepdun roared with an open mouth smile.

Heath nearly jumped completely out of his skin, as did most of the boys watching. But, soon they all joined Steepdun in laughter. Steepdun had a deep roar of a laugh, and he leaned his head straight up at the moon, and slapped his knees. He laughed so hard he started coughing.

"Mates, you shoulda seen the look on your faces," he blurted through his laughs and coughs. "How's your underwear, mate? I bet you nearly soiled yourself, huh?" Steepdun hooted some more.

"Olzfeld is the brand here written on my boots!" Steepdun bellowed.

After hearing his elaborate hoax of a story, and scaring Heath and everyone else half to death, Steepdun won the approval of the entire Salamander cabin. Ricky couldn't tell if he was laughing at the joke, or the joy of the relief knowing it wasn't a true story. Spencer tried to lie and say he knew it was a joke the whole time, then the cabin laughed at him too.

* * *

Once they got back up into the platform to go to bed, the Salamanders resumed their nightly debate over the prettiest girl at camp, and which one each liked the most. The responses became fewer and further apart while one by one they trailed off to sleep. Lying on his mat with no roof over his head, Ricky saw more stars that night than ever before. The haze of the sky revealed the white, scattered stars as far and wide as he could see. It was such a clear night, that he could even see some of the dust and gas of the Milky Way galaxy. He wondered if somewhere out there someone was looking at the same stars, or maybe someone on the other end of those stars was looking up at him. Or maybe, he thought, they were put there just so that he could lay on his back in the cool pale air, that smelled like pine trees and smoke, just for him to look up at them.

"Ahrooo!" Ricky howled like a wolf at the moon.

CHAPTER 21

The Louis Stevens

"Pssstt," whispered Spencer poking Ricky in the shoulder to wake him up. "Psst, Ricky, are you up?"

"No," Ricky moaned back.

"Keep it down," Spencer shushed him. Spencer confirmed everyone else was still asleep on the platform. "Come on man, wake up," Spencer said with urgency in his voice, enough so that Ricky was curious.

"What do you want?" Ricky yawned.

"We need to go back to the cabin."

"No way, why?"

"Shhhh," Spencer signaled. "We'll be back in no time. Let's go."

The desperation in Spencer's voice caused Ricky to sit up a little bit. Ricky checked his watch light to find it was 1:38 am. They whispered so as not to wake anyone else.

"Are you crazy?" Ricky asked.

"Look, I had an accident. I need to go back. Please come with me."

Finally, Ricky understood, "Why should I?"

"Come on man, please. I'd do the same for you," Spencer couldn't say those words with a straight face; he hoped it was dark enough for Ricky not to notice.

"No you wouldn't," Ricky said putting his head back down.

"Come on, please?"

Ricky knew he shouldn't, but he felt sorry for Spencer. He started to wrangle his way out of his sleeping bag and spoke through clenched teeth, "You owe me."

"Keep it down," Spencer murmured.

Spencer and Ricky tiptoed over the wooden platform to the ladder. The structure was so sturdy that it didn't make any creeks while the two boys snuck around, holding their breath the whole way. They each grabbed a flashlight but were too scared to turn them on. After stepping over and around the sleeping campers, they descended the ladders into the dark. It wasn't until they both planted their feet on the ground that they turned on their flashlights, and not until they entered the tree line before either of them spoke.

"So, you peed the bed?" Ricky asked immediately.

"No. Shut up," Spencer pushed at him.

"Hey. I'll go back and leave you here if you do that again," Ricky threatened shining the light on his own face as he said it.

Both of them were scared to be in the woods in the middle of the night, neither wanted to go off alone. So, they avoided calling the other's bluff. They carried on with Ricky leading the way. While they cleared the meadow, the stars and moon lit the sky bright enough that they almost didn't need flashlights. But underneath the tree line, the darkness was so heavy that both boys could practically feel their pupils stretching to get any last drop of light they could find.

"Why'd you pick me anyways?" Ricky asked, knowing the answer.

"Because you know the way," Spencer lied.

"Yeah right, Spencer," Ricky spun around. "You asked me cause you think I'm not going to tell anyone, that's why. Cause I'm nice. And you know it."

Spencer pushed Ricky's flashlight away, "Just keep going, we have to make it there and back before anyone wakes up."

"You smell like pee," Ricky said over his shoulder. "What if you attract a mountain lion or something?"

"No I don't," Spencer mumbled. Ricky could hear from the way Spencer choked on his words that he was about to cry. Ricky knew Spencer asked him for help was because Ricky never teased anyone the way the other guys did. So, when he heard the crack in Spencer's voice, he kept quiet. Spencer sniffled a little and wiped his nose.

"There's probably not any mountain lions out here."

That was as close as Ricky could get to an apology, especially for Spencer.

"Obviously there's no mountain lions," Spencer sniffled. "Idiot."

Since they didn't have Steepdun stopping to point stuff out to them, and they didn't dilly-dally around jumping over boulders or going off the trail, they arrived back at the cabin quicker than expected. Spencer changed out of his sticky shorts in the dark, too scared of getting caught by turning the light on. Ricky stood watch in the doorway and because Spencer called him an idiot when he tried to apologize, Ricky couldn't help but make a few comments about how embarrassed Spencer ought to feel for wetting the bed. Spencer denied peeing his bed was the reason he had to go back and change his shorts.

"Okay Water Boy, it took us an hour to get here. If we hurry back, we'll make it before anyone wakes up, and it will still be dark."

They crept along the shadows of the cabins, back to the forest entrance, making sure to keep their flashlights off and mouths shut. Campers could get in a lot of trouble for sneaking out at night. Neither one wanted to explain to a camp ranger why they were sneaking around after curfew.

Then they saw the lights.

"Get down, get down," Ricky hushed over to Spencer as he ran and ducked around the ledge of the wall lining the main trail.

"Do you see them?" Ricky whispered to Spencer.

About a dozen flashlights bounced their way into the Grand Hall. Spencer and Ricky could practically hear their hearts beating.

"Who is that?" Ricky asked Spencer.

"Those jerks," was all Spencer answered. "We gotta get a little closer."

"Fat chance. Who is that?"

Spencer crawled along the edge, making sure to stay in the shadows and as low as possible, as he approached the Grand Hall.

"Spencer! *Psst* Spencer," Ricky hissed in his loudest whisper. Ricky crouched after him. "Whoever it is, they'll have a lookout."

The warning finally got Spencer to stop dead in his tracks. Spencer explained to Ricky that he was certain the lights up ahead belonged to the eighth graders from Porcupine cabin.

"The eighth grade girls got assigned kitchen duty for the weekend, because the kitchen staff is off for break," Spencer explained.

"Oh yeah, I remember hearing some girls complaining about it at the pool," Ricky connected the dots.

"I bet they're going to prank the eighth grade girls by trashing the place." Spencer guessed. "Dang, that's gonna be a good prank."

"Yeah it kind of is," Ricky agreed. "What should we do?"

"We have to hurry back and tell the guys."

Ricky and Spencer slithered their way in the shadows all the way back down the path towards the trail. Once they knew they were out of sight from the Grand Hall, they turned their flashlights on and booked it. They made it about halfway back to the tower when they saw three flashlights coming from up ahead. Ricky and Spencer ducked off from the trail and waited until the lights got closer, wondering if their own flashlights had been spotted too. It wasn't long before they could hear the voices approaching. They recognized the loudest bickering voice belonged to TJ Stanton, and so Spencer and Ricky turned their flashlights back on to signal to the rest of them. TJ was with Ace and Great Dane.

"TJ remind me to never take you on a spy mission," Spencer spoke loud, confident that they were alone and safe in the darkness of the forest.

"Where the heck did y'all go?" asked Ace.

"Ricky peed his pants and wanted me to go back with him to get a new pair," Spencer blurted out.

It was too dark to see, but Ricky's jaw dropped.

"You did what!" Great Dane laughed loud enough for his voice to echo off the trees.

"I did not! It was Spencer," Ricky rebutted. "Spencer peed the bed; he woke me up and begged me to go with him. He's a lying snake!"

"Shut up, Water Boy," Spencer said putting the flashlight to his face. "Guys listen. We caught the eighth graders trashing the Grand Hall."

"What do you mean?" TJ asked.

"He's lying!" Ricky wasn't ready to change the subject.

"While we were walking back from Aqua Man over here changing his diaper, we saw them going into the Grand Hall," Spencer continued.

"You're a snake Spencer," Ricky snarled. "It wasn't me guys! Look! He's the one wearing different shorts, not me."

"Yo, shut up," Great Dane took charge. "Why they wanna do that?"

"Cause the staff is on break this weekend," Spencer explained.

"So the eighth grade girls will be the ones who have to clean it up," Ricky finished the explanation, still fuming from Spencer's betrayal. "Cause they're on kitchen duty tomorrow."

"Oh, that's rich," Ace laughed.

"Yeah it is," TJ agreed.

"Should we try and stop them?" Ricky asked.

"We have to go wake up the guys," TJ said, trying to take the leadership role back from Great Dane.

When all five of them returned to the sleeping platform, they made zero attempts to be stealthy. Most of the cabin woke up before the last guy climbed the ladder. As the sleeping bags rustled, some boys turned on their flashlights; others looked up, saw the characters involved and went immediately back to bed.

"What's going on?"

"Who's there?"

"Shut up."

"We caught the eighth graders trashing the Grand Hall," TJ spoke at full volume. "Ricky peed his sleeping bag, and tried to cover it up—"

"—It was Spencer!" Ricky interrupted.

TJ continued, ignoring Ricky's outburst, "And while him and Spencer were at the cabin they saw the eighth graders walking into the Grand Hall to trash the place, cause the eighth grade girls have to clean it this weekend."

"That's a pretty good idea," Artie admitted.

"It was Spencer who peed the sleeping bag," Ben Li reported. "I heard him tell Ricky. That's why they left. Ricky's telling the truth."

"Thank you, Ben Li," Ricky said with both hands pointing to Ben Li.

"Who cares about which one of you pissed the bed?" Dez said almost yelling. "Are we going to do anything about the eighth graders?"

"You could do a Louis Stevens," came Heath's voice from across the platform, demanding an instant silence from the arguing campers.

All their flashlights pointed to Heath.

"Do a who?" Artie asked.

"Who's Louis?" Great Dane echoed.

"Amateurs," Heath checked his watch. "Go in there, and clean up the whole thing."

"Oh no. I'm not cleaning nothing," Marcus was out.

"Don't you see?" Heath shook his head. "You guys go in there and clean up the whole thing, then tomorrow morning, the Porcupine guys will walk in expecting to see the reaction from the eighth grade girls, but it'll be clean as a whistle. Think about how disappointed they'll be. And they'll be so pissed off that they're bound to admit they trashed the place just to find out who cleaned it. Plus, word does eventually get out; now all the sudden the eighth grade girls will owe you boys a favor. *That's* a Louis Stevens."

After some debate, they made a unanimous decision to go with the Louis Stevens plan. Heath suggested that they pack up and stop back at Salamander to drop off their stuff, and then sneak into the Grand Hall no later than 4:30 in the morning. The gang agreed it would take commitment, and a team effort to pull it off the right way. Although Health could orchestrate the whole thing, it would be a black ops mission. Meaning, it was high stakes: campers caught out after curfew could suffer serious disciplinarian consequences, and what's more, Heath would be forced to deny any and all knowledge that the prank was going to occur.

Every boy turned his head to see if Steepdun was awake. As a camp ranger, he couldn't be involved in any manner of a prank whatsoever. Steepdun exhaled deeply, sound asleep with his hat pulled over his nose. When the campers wondered if he'd report them after he woke up alone on the platform, he snored and shook his head 'No.'

CHAPTER 22

Pranked

"Hurry up, dudes," Zach Taylor rushed his cabin mates bright and early the next morning. "I want to get there early enough to see the look on their faces."

"Did you guys make sure to hang the toilet paper from the chandeliers?" asked Chuck Schnoll, the Porcupine cabin leader. Chuck was about the same age as Heath, but the two never got along. In fact, Heath tried to avoid Chuck whenever possible.

"Oh man, they'll never be able to get that down. Remember I told you guys to do that, right?" Chuck bragged, looking at himself in the mirror. Chuck decided that he needed to reapply another coat of gel to his blonde tipped spikes. "That toilet paper will be up there for days."

"Oh yeah. We got it all over the chandeliers," Patrick Winkerton replied.

* * *

"Trust me, you guys don't want to get there first," Heath said from sitting up in his bed rubbing his eyes. "Only an amateur shows up early for a prank. The key is to get in there the same time you always do. Don't act suspicious, or you'll blow the whole deal. Be normal."

"Well, I'm starving," said Artie. "Sometimes we get there early."

"True, and I'm hungry too," admitted Heath. "We'll start getting ready and we'll go in a few minutes, did you any of you remember to leave a calling card?"

"Yeah, I left one," TJ assured the cabin. "They had toilet paper on the chandeliers and I left a little piece hanging up there on one of them."

* * *

"I don't believe this," Chuck shook his head as he and his cabin approached the Grand Hall.

A group of fifth grade girls ran into the dining hall ahead of them. When they opened the doors the girls entered as if it was any other morning. The Grand Hall looked exactly the way it always did for breakfast. The Porcupine cabin stood at the entrance dumfounded. Each of them looked to the other for answers.

"How is this possible?"

Zach approached one of the eighth grade girls, Jenna Delgado, for answers. The thin eighth grade girl with long dark brown hair and tan skin examined her nails behind the fruit station. Zach asked her if she knew anything about what was going on.

"Going on with wha*ttt*?" she replied, emphasizing the *T* at the end of *what*.

"When did you guys have to get in here this morning?" Zach asked.

"Just early enough to get all the food out; the chefs were here a little bit before us."

"Did the chefs say anything to you about anything being out of the ordinary?" Zach asked.

"I don't talk to the chefs." Jenna looked annoyed, and she had no idea why Zach was getting upset.

When the Salamander cabin strolled in, they looked tired and zombie-like with bedhead and wrinkled clothes, as they always did. For anyone observing the seventh grade boys, it appeared to be business as usual. But the Salamanders kept sharp eyes and ears for anything going on out of the ordinary. Their curiosity and pride of a perfectly executed prank could only be contained so much.

Back at the eighth grade boys' table, they continued to be perplexed. Most of the guys had similar conversations as Zach with other eighth grade girls, but not one of them had anything to report. *Maybe the chefs cleaned it*, they thought. But if the chefs walked into a messy kitchen, the whole world would have known about it, and they certainly would report a mess to the camp rangers. The camp rangers woulda had every student lined up against the wall for an interrogation. No; the chefs definitely didn't clean the mess.

Chuck slammed his hands on the table and got up to discuss the issue with Nicole Nensworth, the eighth grade girls' cabin leader. Perhaps she could help them get to the bottom of it. Nicole was the perfect candidate for the eighth grade girls' cabin leader. She was a collegiate volleyball player, beautiful, tall, and intimidating. Both the Salamander and Porcupine cabins spent most nights debating whether Nicole or Brittney was the most beautiful person in the world. Chuck walked with his hands held out to his sides showing Nicole both of his palms.

"What's going on in here today?" Chuck asked, standing eye level to Nicole's chin.

Nicole rolled her eyes, so that she spoke looking away from Chuck, "What do you want, Chuck?"

"Oh come on, I know it was you," he said, resting one hand against the wall. Nicole crossed her arms.

"What. Was. Me?"

Chuck pressed his lips and raised his eyebrows together, then jutted his chin out towards her, "Come on. Seriously? Just tell me. It was my guys who did it. How'd you girls get this turned around so fast?"

"Chuck, what the heck are you talking about? You're bothering me."

"You really don't know?"

"No. I have no idea what you're talking about, and I don't want to." She rolled her eyes again, this time back towards Chuck and gave him a vicious stare. "Are we done?"

Chuck bobbed his head a few times, "Okay, okay, I believe you." He said backpedaling.

"Thanks, bye," Nicole waived.

Heath watched the exchange from the table. He couldn't hear them, but he didn't need to, he knew exactly what they were saying. While Chuck sulked over to his table, his shoulders rolled forward and the spikes in his blond hair wilting, Ricky nudged TJ to look over at Nolan, who was pointing up at the single piece of toilet paper hanging from the chandeliers. The Salamander table exchanged smiles over their rival's frustration.

"What the heck?" Nolan said looking up to the chandeliers. "Somebody in here knows! And I want to find out who it is!"

"Me too," Patrick slammed his spoon into his cereal. They shouted at each other loud enough for the Salamanders, and most of the cafeteria to hear.

Sensing trouble, Camp Ranger Howard hurried over with his clipboard in hand.

"Good morning boys, what's the matter this morning?" he asked.

"Nothing," Patrick answered wiping some of the milk he splashed on the table.

"Seems to be quite a bit of commotion over here if you ask me. Enjoying your breakfast?" Ranger Howard investigated.

"Someone in here is lying; that's what," Zach Taylor announced. He scanned the dinning hall to try and figure out who had tried to get the best of him.

Before anyone could answer, Jenna tapped the camp ranger on the shoulder, "Do you know where any of the mops are? I can't find them and someone spilled."

"Oh cram it, Jenna!" Zach couldn't take it anymore. He stood up, face cherry red, and stomped over to her.

"Mr. Taylor," Ranger Howard held out his hand signaling a halt.

Zach shouted so loudly that most of the campers stopped to look over at the scene, none enjoying it more than the Salamander table.

"She's a liar!" Zach screamed again pointing at her. "They're all liars! We know what you did."

"Eww. You are psycho," Jenna sassed back, moving her upper body like a cobra.

This brought Nicole to the table to join the argument. "What's going on over here?" Nicole chimed in.

Chuck stood up and put his hands on Zach's shoulder, "Okay, listen buddy. Sorry Ranger Howard. Zach is just a little upset."

"What are you talking about, you creep?" Jenna asked.

"Chill out, dude," Patrick whispered to Zach.

"What is wrong with you and your cabin today, Chuck?" she pointed her index finger at him.

"Oh, like you don't already know?" Chuck replied at full volume. "Your whole stinkin' cabin should get an Academy Award for this performance."

"Excuse me. Mr. Schnoll," interrupted Ranger Howard. "That's no way to talk to another cabin leader."

"Yes, I'm sorry sir. Sorry Nicole. We had a long night in our cabin; I think everyone is just a little cranky this morning."

"I want to know what's going on," Nicole demanded.

"Me too!" shouted Jenna.

"As do I," Ranger Howard said clicking his pen getting ready to write a report.

The eighth grad boys sat at their table silent. Meanwhile the Salamanders had their shirts over their mouths unable to control their giggles.

"If I can't get an explanation in the next minute, I will revoke blob privileges for the entire eighth grade boys cabin."

"You already did that," Nolan blurted.

"Then I'll take away your go-kart privileges too."

"For what? We didn't do anything!" Zach screamed.

The words echoed through the entire cafeteria.

"It's nothing sir, honest," Nolan stood up to explain. "We just had a misunderstanding. We thought we got pranked by the girls last night," he said looking as innocent as a lamb, with peanut butter on the sides of his mouth.

"Well, we didn't do anything," Jenna huffed at Zach.

"I don't buy it." Ranger Howard leaned over the table, making sure each eighth grade boy had the opportunity to stare at himself through the reflection of his sunglasses. When the lenses stopped over Patrick Winkerton, he momentarily looked up at the chandelier over their table. Ranger Howard's gaze jolted upward and he spotted the toilet paper strand. Uncertain how or why it got there, it revealed enough; *something* was going on.

"I'm revoking the go-kart privileges, effective immediately."

The entire cafeteria gasped, except the Salamanders, their laughs grew louder.

"For how long?" Zach winced.

"Until further notice," Ranger Howard grunted. "Good day," and he stomped off.

"But we didn't do anything!" Patrick yelped, face red and eyes full of water.

"We got a crier!" Spencer couldn't help himself.

The whole cafeteria laughed at Patrick, Zach, Nolan, and the rest of the Porcupines.

The seventh graders beamed with pride of the job they did. They handled themselves perfectly under the pressure, given the circumstances. After the eighth grader's go-kart privileges were revoked, Ricky realized he played a pivotal role in pulling off one of the all-time greatest pranks in the history of Camp Tallawanda.

"We're going to find out who messed with us," Zach promised his goons. "Somebody around here knows something. And when we find out, they'll be sorry."

CHAPTER 23

Battle Ready

"Because it will be good practice for you guys," Heath explained standing in the center of Cooke Field.

After pulling off the Louis Stevens, the Salamanders dedicated themselves to improving their lacrosse game. Embarrassing the eighth graders in front of the whole camp, and causing friction between them and the eighth grade girls was an act of war. The Salamanders knew it would end in a battle on the lacrosse field. They'd have to be ready.

"We need practice," Heath went on.

"How is beating up on some sixth grade scrubs going to help us?" Spencer asked.

"So you know what it will feel like to stop a shot?" Ben Li suggested.

"I think it will be fun," Ricky inputted. "What time are they coming over?"

"They're coming now," TJ pointed.

"Alright, listen up. Bring it in," Heath yelled, and the team obeyed. "I don't care about these sixth graders any more than you do. But I want to watch you guys working our offense. Move the ball around, fight for ground balls, and take good shots. That's what good teams do. Got it?"

They nodded.

The sixth grade cabin hardly put up a fight against the mighty Salamanders. Their afternoons spent practicing showed through good communication and crisp passes. Ricky had come a long way too. He understood the game and maneuvered with and without the ball like he'd been playing lacrosse for years.

With Heath's coaching, Ricky and the others perfected the two-triangle offense. Heath drew it up like this:

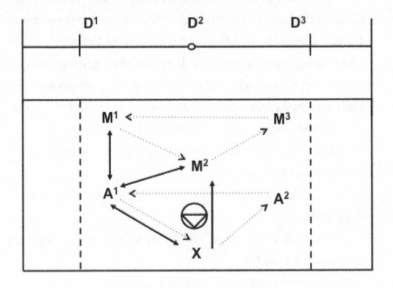

The triangle offense focused on movement. As Heath explained, Midfielder-1 passes it down to Attack-1, and then

Midfielder-1 follows his pass into the crease. Midfielder-2 rotates to top right, and Midfielder-3 shifts across to reset the top triangle. It was the same motion for the attacks. Attack-1 could feed Midfielder-2, or pass the ball to X. The attack should always motion the triangle to follow his pass, or run the ball down to become the new X. The triangles could move in either direction at any time. The constant moving parts eventually confused a defense and left someone open for a quick shot.

However, it was of the utmost importance that someone maintained the X position. If a shot soared too wide or too high from the goal and out of bounds, the closest team to the ball when it goes out of bounds gains possession. So, as long as there was a player positioned at X standing behind the goal, the Salamanders stayed on offense after a high or wide shot.

"Keep moving, rotate the points!" Heath ordered from the sidelines.

Despite his progress, Ricky watched the first possession from the bench. Just as he watched the eighth graders during that first scrimmage several weeks ago, he witnessed his own team maneuver their offense with ease against the younger opponents. Ace won the face-off and tossed the ball down to Dez. Dez ran it behind the goal to X, and then whipped it back up to Marcus on the right side. Marcus reversed the triangle and took the ball back to the X position, causing Dez to rotate up and to the left. Ben Li crashed down from the crease, and Marcus passed it to him for a front dead-center goal.

"This. Game's. Over!" Artie shouted from the sidelines.

Ben Li rarely celebrated, but he openly accepted the hugs and cheers from the rest of his teammates on the field. After the quick goal, Ben jogged off the field signaling for Ricky to sub in. Ace wasn't able to win the face-off as cleanly the second time, so he had to kick the ball over to Ricky. Ricky dropped one knee low, and put his face directly over the ball, the way Heath told him to, and scooped it. Ricky adjusted his grip to switch the stick over to his left hand, and sprinted past the slow sixth grade defender trying to swing at him. Marcus whizzed by his defender and ran wide open. He shouted to Ricky calling for the pass. Ricky saw Marcus, but wanted to show the guys how much he improved. Instead of passing it to his open teammate, Ricky ripped a hard shot with a defender in front of him. Somehow, the ball still found its way into the back of the net.

"Nice shot Ricky," a familiar voice shouted from the sidelines. Claire arrived to watch the game with Danielle and a two of their friends. She waived to Ricky; he nodded back, hoping she couldn't see his giant smile through his helmet.

"Can I take this face off?" Ricky asked Ace.

"Why?"

"I don't know. Claire's over there."

"Hey partner, you tryin' to strut your stuff? Be my guest," Ace said backing away.

Ricky won the face-off, sprinted down the field. Marcus again managed to get himself wide open and called for the ball, but Ricky ignored him. He spun around a defender and belted another shot for his second goal.

"Show off!" Great Dane clapped from the far defensive end.

Ricky put his hands over his head wheezing to get some fresh air in his burning lungs. He gestured for Ben to go back in for him. The other boys on the sidelines gave him high-fives and fist bumps for his two goals. Ricky held his chin high on his way towards the water bottles. He took his helmet off with one hand to talk to Claire.

"Didn't see you there," Ricky lied, unable to hide his grin.

"Sure you didn't. Only one more for the hat-trick," Claire winked.

What's a hat-trick? Ricky asked himself, embarrassed to admit Claire knew another sports word he'd never heard of.

"Hey Romeo," Heath called from center field. "Come here."

Ricky expected to get congratulated on his two goals, but Heath looked as mad as he did the day he saved Artie's life.

"Listen buddy," Heath rested his hands on his knees and stared at Ricky. "What you just did out there was selfish. It's easy to score against these little sixth graders, but if you tried doing that against Porcupine, that's leaving points off the board. Do you understand? When you've got a guy wide-open—especially Marcus—your job is to pass him the ball. Got it?"

"Yeah, I'm sorry," Ricky's stomach started to knot.

"Hey, it's just a scrimmage," Heath gently whacked Ricky's chest. "And those were good shots, but lacrosse is a team game. Don't forget that."

"I know, I'm sorry," Ricky lowered his head. "I just wanted everyone to see I got better."

"Yeah don't worry about that. *She* saw alright," Heath laughed. "Don't forget what I told you. Now. Let her see you get the hat-trick."

Ricky's expressionless face told Heath he didn't understand.

"That's three goals in one game, Rick," Heath winked.

The rest of the game went by as easily as it started. The Salamander cabin proved that sacrificing most of their afternoons from the zip line or go-karts did not go to waste. They beat the sixth graders 16-2. The Salamanders focused their sights on a rematch with the Porcupines.

CHAPTER 24

Summer Dance | Dinner with Dale and Marsha

Of course it would be on the same night. That was just Ricky's luck. No chance his parents would let him have *that* much fun. The most anticipated night of the summer arrived. Camp Tallawanda prepared for its annual Summer Ball for the seventh and eighth graders. It would be just like a school dance, but the major difference being that instead of watchful chaperoning teachers eyeing every move, the Summer Ball was supervised by college-aged cabin leaders and camp staff, all of whom had their own social distractions to worry about. It would be a prime opportunity for campers to give and receive their first kiss. Ricky devastated Claire when he told her that his parents were going to be coming up for the weekend. He couldn't go to the dance.

The Salamander cabin teased Ricky relentlessly when he broke the news about his parents' surprise early visit.

"Don't worry," Spencer sneered. "Once Zach Taylor is done dancing with Hannah, he'll save a kiss for Claire too!"

Spencer's insult hurt the most, but there were others. Mostly it was TJ telling him to get out from living in his parents' bubble. Dane asked if Ricky planned to slow dance with his mom, which got a lot of laughs. But mainly, they just teased him for missing out on another fun part of the summer and a crucial checkpoint for starting junior high in the fall.

Then the discussion moved away from Ricky and on to first kisses: who had one, who didn't, and the likelihood they'd be going around all night at the dance. Ricky never kissed a girl before, and he hoped it would have happened that night. But thanks to his parents, that would be impossible.

"Oh man, definitely at a first dance," TJ explained. "Anyone who isn't a total loser is guaranteed to kiss a girl at the first dance."

They argued for a long time about the mechanics of the whole ordeal.

"No, y'all," Ace lectured. "That's called a French kiss, that's the real deal."

"What is a French kiss?" Ben asked.

"Ben Li, are you kidding me?" Spencer howled. "You don't know?"

"Oh come on Spencer, you don't know either," Marcus huffed.

"I know what it is," said Artie proudly. "It's when you play tonsil hockey."

"Okay, and what the heck is that?" asked Dez.

Artie didn't know.

"Okay, guys cut it out. There'll be no kissing on my watch," Heath promised.

"Dude," said Great Dane. "Only thing you gonna be watchin' tonight is Brittney."

Ricky watched and listened with envy as he got dressed for a long night out to dinner with his parents. Mr. and Mrs. Collins planned to take him into town. Ricky did the math, the drive into town would be about a thirty-minutes, plus dinner, plus whatever else they'd have in store for him. No chance he'd make it back in time for the dance. The boys talked about slow dancing, and girls, and kissing, and Ricky would have given his new wooden lacrosse stick to be able to be there with them.

"Have fun with your mommy and daddy," they snickered as he headed out the door to the Camp Commissioner's Office to get picked up.

During the lonely walk to the office, Ricky had to fight off tears when we saw the lights decorating the outdoor dance-floor. He heard Chuck doing a sound check with music equipment. Chuck waived, but Ricky didn't bother waving back. When he finally made it up to the front office entrance, Ricky was about to put his hand on the doorknob when the door swung open.

"Boy, I sure do feel sorry for you tonight," Margaret said chomping her gum and indicating for him to sit on the porch outside of the office. Margaret had her hair in such a tight ponytail Ricky wondered if it hurt her forehead. She spun around to show off her pink and black old fashioned, 1950's poodle skirt.

"Your parents will be here any minute, and they better be quick," Margaret said locking the door. "I got to stay here with you 'till they get here, then it's party time for me." Margaret explained shaking her hips and snapping her fingers in uncoordinated and rickety movements.

"You're going to the dance too?"

"Of course I am," she started dancing like a rusty robot. "Best night of the summer. If you were lucky, I was going to save you a dance."

Ricky shrugged and put his head down.

"What's the matter, Casanova?"

Ricky didn't answer; he could feel the tingling behind his eyes, and the tightness growing around his chest. If he answered, he was afraid he'd cry.

"Oh look, so you're missing the dance; big deal," Margaret sat next to him. "Look if it means that much to you, come up to the office sometime, I'll turn the radio on and you can get your dance with me, okay?"

This made Ricky laugh a little bit.

"I'm technically not supposed to know about any of this: But between you and me," Margaret looked around to make sure no one was listening, and she leaned in to whisper to him with her hand covering her mouth.

"The best part of the dance happens after the dance," Margaret leaned back, raised her eyebrows and thumped Ricky's chest with her backhand. "Know what I'm saying?"

She tapped him again and continued to raise her eyebrows, "You get what I'm saying?"

"Not really," Ricky half smiled.

"I'm saying go to dinner with your parents, just make sure you get back here in time to figure out the plans for after the dance. That's usually when the campers have the most fun ... but you didn't hear that from me," Margaret gave a long exaggerated wink with her blue eye shadow.

Just when Ricky started feeling better, his parents' car arrived. Margaret slapped him on the knee and got up to walk away. She didn't say a word to his parents.

Mrs. Collins ran out of the car with outstretched arms, taking about six inches with every step, "Oh my goodness, Richard, I've missed you so much. Come here, come here."

"Mom are you crazy? Stop it," Ricky had to pry himself out from his mother's grips before anyone at camp saw her affectionate display.

"Hey, Son," Mr. Collins said, going around the car to shut the door Mrs. Collins left open. He gave Ricky a normal hug, "We missed you."

"Hi, Dad. Missed you too."

"What's the matter?" Mrs. Collins asked.

"I just kind of wanted to go to that dance—"

"—Oh nonsense," Mr. Collins interrupted. "All that sort of shenanigans isn't right for someone your age."

"What do you want to do?" Mrs. Collins asked. "You want to go and dance with girls? You can dance with a girl at your wedding. We didn't send you up here to dance with girls; you're too young."

Ricky looked around, suddenly very thankful for how far away and secluded the Commissioner's Office was from the other camp buildings. Hopefully, no one could hear this bickering. If he got into the car, at least they'd have the argument in private.

"He's not going," Mr. Collins reasoned. "We're here, and that's that. We made dinner reservations. Now, who's hungry?"

Ricky looked out the window while his parents, mostly his mother, rained questions upon him. As usual, Ricky's mother asked questions but didn't bother waiting to hear Ricky's answer before she'd ask another one. Sometimes, she asked questions, then answered them herself.

"How is camp? Have you been eating? Do you miss us? I know you do, I can tell you do. When I talked to you on the phone the other day, I could tell you were homesick. Do you want to come home? Have you made any new friends? I hope you haven't been paling around with that TJ Stanton all summer. Something about that kid, I think he's a troublemaker. What about that Spencer Lutz boy? He has very nice parents. I want to invite him and his family over when you get back. Do you like the food?"

And so on.

"Where are we going?" Ricky asked, noticing they drove past the exit for the closest town.

"We're going to the next town over. It's a little further but we think it's nicer," Mr. Collins explained.

Ricky sunk in his chair. It would be just like his parents to drag this dinner out for as long as possible. He wondered how the guys were doing at the dance.

* * *

"Whoa look at the lights!" Marcus awed.

The camp rangers, cabin leaders, and camp staff helped to transform the fields by the volleyball pits into an outdoor courtyard. Ricky had seen the lights during the day, but he would have been even more depressed if he saw them sparkling in the dark of night. The white strings of Christmas lights stretched over the dance floor glowing like low stars. They even wrapped around the nearby trees and the speaker stands. Most girls waited all summer to debut their nicest dresses, saved for this specific occasion. Girls like Hannah Havinghurst and her eighth grade counterpart, Jenna Delgado, spent literally the entire day getting ready for the dance.

As was to be expected with such events, the boys gathered in small circles and huddles on one side of the dance floor, while the girls did the same on the other side, leaving a wide unoccupied space in the middle. Chuck made a few announcements letting everyone know about the available snacks at front of the stage, and he cracked a joke about spiking the punch, that nobody understood. Standing behind the DJ booth, Chuck was the only person dancing.

Artie, Ben Li, and Spencer made their way to the snacks. They carefully avoided eye contact with any girls, and the girls made sure to avoid them. The only interaction between any males with any females was between the cabin leaders, who paid no attention to the campers. Chester Steepdun was one of the few camp rangers in attendance. Steepdun, Heath, and the sixth grade cabin boys' leader stood in the back corner talking about lacrosse.

"Hey, Mr. DJ," Margaret sang to Chuck as she entered the middle void of the dance-floor. "Play me somethin' groovy."

Chuck fired up an old song from the 90's; Margaret started dancing terribly to it. Margaret danced in her poodle skirt as if she was trying to imitate some sort of circus animal choking to death, or an alien cyborg screwing in a light bulb; no one was sure. But her awful dance moves were enough to cause campers and cabin leaders alike, to slowly trickle closer to the center of the dance floor. Then, a few eighth grade girls jumped in and started dancing with Margaret. Soon after, Nolan and Patrick in matching long sleeve collared shirts, swayed their way into the middle, followed by Zach Taylor and several other eighth grade boys. Eventually, some of the seventh graders even gave in to the gravity of people joining the center. Before the song was over, the middle void of the dance-floor had disappeared.

After a few more fun and upbeat songs, Chuck played the night's first slow song. Dane found the lanky Paige Bacco immediately, and led her to the dance floor. Couples paired off quickly under the lights.

TJ approached Danielle Camina, acknowledging she existed for the first time that week and said, "I guess it's a slow song."

"Was that a question?" she responded.

TJ put his hand out, "Do you want to or not?"

Danielle didn't answer but she let TJ put his arms around her waist, and she rested her arms on his shoulders. They were as close as if they were hugging. When their foreheads started touching each other, Brittney Cannon walked up to them and squeezed her hands in between them. "Remember to leave room for the Holy Spirit," she said.

If anyone was more disappointed about him missing the dance than Ricky, it was Claire Minnich. An eighth grade boy who wasn't very popular with the girls his own age, asked her to dance. She politely shook her head and said she was sorry, but she promised her first dance to be with someone else. She spent most of the night by the snacks with Karen Laund, the girls' goalie, talking with Spencer and Artie.

"Are you going to ask anyone to dance," Dez asked Ace.

"Sure am," Ace said sniffing his breath, and popping a mint into his mouth. "Jenna Delgado."

"What?" Dez's jaw drooped. "Have you lost your mind? She's an eighth grader. The hottest one."

"Well, the way I see it," Ace explained rubbing his hands through his slicked hair. "Jerk bag Zach Taylor an' them

Porcupine goons is focused on goin' after seventh grade girls. Means them poor pretty eighth grade bells are left to their lonesome." Ace winked. "Opportunity is knockin', Dez. I'm fixin' to answer."

Before Dez could respond, Ace walked in a straight line to Jenna Delgado, and the rest of the most popular eighth grade girls' circle. Dez couldn't believe it. Ace took Jenna by the hand and lead her to the dance floor. He stood with his hands on Jenna's hips, and Dez's eyes popped when Jenna put her arms on Ace's shoulders. They rocked slowly side to side, and then Ace pulled her in a little closer.

It wasn't long before the rest of the Salamander cabin spotted Ace. Any of the Salamander guys who weren't dancing with a girl, which was practically all of them, gathered around Dez to try and figure out how it happened. Dez shook his head in disbelief.

"He just went up there and asked her," Dez tried to explain. "Craziest thing I've ever seen."

"Like a Jedi mind trick?" suggested Ben Li.

"Can't score if you don't shoot," Marcus commented in disbelief.

Ace and Jenna danced and slowly spun so that now Jenna's back was to Dez and the rest of the guys. Ace stared right at them grinning ear to ear. As the song was about to end, Ace slid his hands down passed Jenna's floral printed hips, and with both hands, he took a full squeeze.

Jenna pushed him away shouting, "You creep!" She stomped off back towards her friends. "Don't touch me!" she shrieked at him once she got further away.

* * *

In the restaurant, Ricky sat on one side of the booth while his parents sat across from him, like a job interview. He couldn't stop thinking about how much fun the guys were probably having, and he hoped no one was dancing with Claire. Ricky worried if Spencer was right, and maybe Zach Taylor would be dancing with both Hannah and Claire throughout the night. After they sat down at the first table, his mother thought it was too drafty near the window, and she requested that they'd be moved, which took awhile.

"What do you want?" Mrs. Collins asked looking at the menu.

"I want to be back at camp and go to the dance," Ricky mumbled.

"Enough Rick," Mr. Collins said handing him a menu. "Don't make a scene."

Ricky barely touched his food. What felt like several hours later, when the meal eventually ended, Mr. Collins tried to pay with a coupon. Unfortunately, the coupon was for a different restaurant that had a similar name. This took even more time to sort out. Mr. Collins insisted that the waitress let him use it anyways. It was then that she pointed out it was expired. That's when Ricky's dad asked to speak with the manager.

* * *

From the beginning of the first slow song to the end of the night, Dane and Paige slow danced with each other. Somehow, Ace convinced Jenna to let him dance with her again, which was the result of a well-crafted apology, persistence, and the lack of any other boys having enough courage to ask her. Poor Claire Minnich, she went off and hid in the bathroom during the slow songs, because the boy she'd been hoping for weeks to dance with, was out at some restaurant with his parents two towns away.

"Oh man, y'all are going to love this," Ace prefaced, walking up towards TJ, Dez, and Marcus, looking for some more congratulations after another slow song.

"How did you pull that off man?" Dez asked.

"Yeah, who do you think you are?" TJ followed up.

"I'm the guy who just set us up with a little rendezvous at the lake," Ace bragged.

"For what?" TJ asked.

"I think they wanna go skinny dippin'," Ace said stone faced.

"Jenna Delgado wants to go skinny dipping! With us?" Marcus bounced as he spoke.

The boys oohed and ahhed at the news, but Ace explained it was to be of the highest level of secrecy. No one else could know. Jenna told him he could only bring three friends. They swore they wouldn't tell anyone else, and Ace laid out the rest of the details in a whisper.

CHAPTER 25

Midnight at the Lake

"Why would you want to go back to the cabin?" Mrs. Collins asked. "It's so far, and it's already so late, stay at the hotel with us. We'll drive you back in the morning."

"Yeah, that's too long of a drive, and it's so late. We'll take you in the morning," Mr. Collins agreed.

"We're going to the hotel. What do you want to do back at camp?" Mrs. Collins went on, "There's nothing going on there at this hour; everyone's going to sleep."

Ricky took a few deep breaths through his nose before he answered, "Yeah! Of course! It's the summer dance; I wanted to go. I'm not a bad kid because I wanted to go to the dance."

"Richard, we didn't want you going to that dance," Marsha turned around to explain.

"Duh!" Ricky said through a red face, "Obviously you didn't want me going, you guys never want me doing anything and you know what, Mom? Sometimes you guys are wrong."

"Come on now, Rick," his dad answered first. "Calm down."

"No. It's not fair. You guys knew the dance was tonight, and you came down here to sabotage me, and you were wrong for doing it."

"We let you go to camp, didn't we?" Mr. Collins asked, squeezing the wheel a little tighter.

"Yeah you did, eventually-after I begged all night! Is this how it's going to be for the rest of my life? I have to fight and beg with you every time I want to do anything?"

"Ricky nobody does everything," his dad explained. "Sometimes in life you're going to miss out on stuff."

"That's fine, but I shouldn't have to beg for the rest of my life *every* time I want to do something, right?" Ricky slammed his back against the seat. "Is that how you two grew up?"

The sound of the rotating tires filed the silence in the car. Mr. and Mrs. Collins exchanged a glance in the front seat.

"Maybe you're right, Richard," Mrs. Collins said quietly.

"I am right. But now I'm stuck in the car with you two when I should be at the most fun night of camp," Ricky huffed. "You guys basically kidnapped me."

Both of Ricky's parents started laughing. Despite how upset he was, Ricky couldn't hide his smile in the backseat.

"He's right, Dale," Mrs. Collins laughed, "We didn't want him to go to the dance, so we kidnapped our own son from summer camp. We're sorry, Richard."

"Should we head back?" Mr. Collins offered. "It really is a little too late for that now, son. We're sorry."

As Ricky sat in the backseat, he felt a little better, but had no real options; it was too late to go back that night. His imagination went wild with all the fun he'd be missing. He worried most about Claire. Maybe she'd find a new boy from the cabin. Maybe she'd like the other guy better than him, or maybe an eighth grader. He wondered if the Salamanders were making fun of him behind his back. When he got back in the morning he'd find out he was the only guy in the whole cabin who didn't have a first kiss. Ricky didn't let his parents hear, but he cried himself to sleep that night in the hotel. This wasn't how he was supposed to spend his first junior high dance.

* * *

Ace led the way. At 11:50 pm, he got out of his bunk as quietly as he could and walked into the bathroom. He was the first to climb out the window. TJ, Dez, and Marcus snuck out behind him.

"What if we get caught?" Dez worried.

"Are you kidding me?" Marcus whispered back, as they slunk along the shadows to the far end of the lake. "Do you realize what kind of golden opportunity this is? Some guys go their whole life without skinning dipping at a lake."

"Shut up," TJ whispered. "We can't get caught before we get there."

According to TJ's calculations, there was a 100% chance that they'd be going skinny-dipping. TJ theorized that the eighth grade girls were fed up with the Porcupine guys, and they'd be the chosen seventh graders to reap the benefits. As they made their way around the furthest corner from the boy's cabin, they could hear high-pitched feminine giggles up ahead.

"Psst! Ace, we're over here."

Sure enough, Jenna made good on her promise. Four other girls, just barely visible with their heads popping out of the water bobbed waiting for them. The light from the dock flickered across the placid water and cast a deep shadow that the girls seemed to be using for cover. The boys stood at the edge of the lake, staring out at the girls ten yards out into the water. Nothing but the silhouettes of their heads and shoulders were visible in the dark.

"I died and went to heaven," Marcus whispered to his friends.

"Well guys? Let's get in," Dez squealed.

"Wait," Jenna stopped them raising her arm out of the water. "Can't you see our stuff?"

A big pile of clothes, sandals, towels, and even bathing suits sat on the ground at the edge of the dock. The guys were so fixated on the voices and getting to the water, they walked right by without noticing.

"Man, are you serious?" Ace whispered. "They're really doing it?"

"If we're doing it, you have to do it too," Jenna said from the water.

"How do we know you're not tricking us?" TJ asked.

Jenna raised herself out of the water. It was dark, much too dark to see anything, but the boys were certain she definitely wasn't wearing a bathing suit. The boys looked around, unsure and insecure about what they should do. Ace didn't hesitate; he threw off his shirt and shoes and waddled into the water.

"Don't come any closer until you take off *everything*," Jenna said. "It has to be fair."

Once Ace was deep enough to cover his waist, he threw his bathing suit out at TJ, and laughed. "Come on guys, are you scared?"

Dez looked to TJ and Marcus to take the lead. Not wanting an opportunity for the other to look like the leader, TJ and Marcus walked into the water together, and removed their swim trunks. Dez followed, laughing the whole way. Once they waddled deep enough, they threw their bathing suits on to the shore. Then they swam out towards the girls.

"Hey Jenna," Ace's voice cracked. "Best day of my life."

"Nope, it's not," said Jenna, and she stood up to reveal that she was indeed wearing a bathing suit. The other girls lifted themselves out of the water to reveal they were all wearing their bathing suits.

"Hey you little jerks!" an unknown fifth voice shouted from the shoreline. Whoever it was, she had her arms full of all the boys' stuff.

"Hey!" Dez splashed.

"Oh come on!" TJ screamed, not worried about getting in trouble. "That's my stuff!"

The boys looked around at each other in a panic. The girls swam over to the edge of the dock and climbed out of the water with the ladder, all of them wearing bathing suits. The boys were stuck in the lake, completely naked.

"Jenna!" Ace shouted. "Come on Jenna, please."

"Sorry Ace," Jenna laughed. "Maybe at the next dance, you'll know how to treat a lady."

"Isn't this against the law or something?" TJ begged.

"Oh Ace, you're such an idiot," Marcus splashed at him.

"How the heck is this my fault?" Ace shivered in the water. "Jenna, come on, man."

"Sorry, Ace," Jenna blew a kiss after she wrapped her towel around herself.

"But we cleaned up the Grand Hall for you!" TJ argued. "And this is the thanks we get?"

"You did what?" Jenna asked.

"We cleaned the Grand Hall after the Porcupines trashed the place, so y'all wouldn't have to," Ace confessed.

"Is that true?" the girl holding the boys' clothes asked.

"Yes," Dez whined. "The eighth grade guys trashed the Grand Hall, and we cleaned it so no one would know."

"Remember? That's the day they got upset in the lunchroom and lost their blob privileges," Marcus explained.

"We did you girls a favor. So give us our clothes back," TJ begged. "Please."

Suddenly the eighth grade girls realized why the Porcupine boys had been acting so strange ever since that morning in the cafeteria. Jenna and the other girls thought about it for a while, and decided to give the boys their shoes and t-shirts only. Then they ran off, leaving them stranded in the water, cold, confused, and naked.

"That was a pretty good prank," Ace admitted with just his head sticking out of the water.

"Great idea, Ace," TJ splashed.

"Man, how the heck was I s'posed to know that was gonna happen?" he splashed back.

"That's what you get for your stunt at the dance," Marcus told him.

"At least they left our shoes," Dez said.

The four of them laughed and complained the whole way back to their cabin. They had to stick their legs through the armholes of their t-shirts and hold them up scrunched around their waists. As they waddled back to Salamander, they bumped into Heath. Heath was just as surprised and embarrassed to the see the nearly naked boys as they were to see him.

Heath shook his head at the four shivering campers and said, "I don't know. I don't want to know. You didn't see me, and I didn't see you. Got it?"

They nodded and he disappeared into the dark.

CHAPTER 26

An Act of War

All eyes in the Sunday afternoon lunchroom followed Zach, Nolan, and Patrick as they marched towards the Salamander table. Zach, conveniently wearing a sleeveless shirt, flexed his sunburnt arms the whole way. Patrick kept his chin high and jaw clenched. Nolan, the slob, had mustard on the corner of his mouth.

"We found out about your little prank," Zach pressed his hands on the table, leaning over and making eye contact with everyone.

"What prank?" Spencer asked. Some of the boys at the table laughed.

"Yeah, yeah, laugh it up," Zach egged them on. "You losers proud of yourselves? Getting our blob privileges taken away? Think you deserve an award for your little clean up job? Well it's coming."

That's all he said.

Zach pushed off from the table, took Spencer's fork out of his macaroni and dropped it on the ground. Patrick jerked his head at Ace, as if he was about to pounce on him, but that was all. With the warning issued, the goons walked away. The Salamanders sat silently for a moment, all of them not quite sure what just happened.

"Wow Spencer, you really wimped out back there," TJ said to Spencer and everyone chuckled.

They hid their nervousness behind the laughter, but they all knew the bullies would not let a prank go unpunished. Something was coming, and whatever it was, it wouldn't be good. They eyed each other in anticipation for the worst.

* * *

"What should we do to them?" Nolan asked on their way back to their own lunch table.

"Don't worry, I got a plan," Zach promised Nolan and Patrick. "We'll show those losers what happens when they try and mess with us."

* * *

When the sevenths graders got back to their cabin from afternoon practice, Ricky noticed it was missing.

"It's not here," he shouted, frantically rummaging through his trunk, pulling out all his clothes, and emptying the drawers. "It's not here!"

"Chill out man," TJ tried grabbing Ricky from the trunk. "What are you looking for?"

"My stick! My wooden stick! I kept in my trunk and its not here."

"Are you sure you had it?" Dez asked.

"Yes! I keep it right here under my sweatshirt!"

Ricky scoured the entire cabin. He opened everyone's trunks and dug through them looking for his stick. Some of the guys joined in peeking under beds to help.

"It ain't here, partner," Ace told him.

"Oh no," Artie shouted from the back room. "Guys, Ricky. Come back here!"

Artie pointed to the stick propped on the table. Ricky recognized the plastic gold that encased his stick. They screwed it into one of the trophy platforms from the fifth grade crafts' class. The screws caused the wood to split apart, and the gold casing seeped into the cracks. The plastic mold even clogged the mesh pocket and gutwall, and hid the engraving of its name. The gold coating lay uneven across the stick and spilled over the edges onto the platform, giving away that the deed was done in a hurry. A note taped to the side of the stick said, *Loser's Award*.

"Oh man, Rick," TJ gave Ricky a pat on the back. "They shouldn't have done that."

Ricky's face burned red, his chest boiled and the hairs and goosebumps on his arms shot up. Some of the guys around him started shouting, and some swore vengeance against Zach Taylor and the rest of the eighth graders. Ricky blocked out their noise. He stood motionless at his stick, and the ugly trophy it became. It was ruined.

"That's messed up, dude," Dane agreed. "What you gonna do?"

Zach Taylor had gone too far. Without a word, Ricky steamed out the door. The rest of Salamander cabin chased after him.

"Fight!" Spencer yelled as they hurried off the steps and down the trail, straight in the direction to Porcupine Cabin.

"Fight!" most of the boys repeated.

As the entire Salamander crew booked it down the main trail of the camp, the commotion attracted several onlookers. Rumors of a fight spread instantly, and camp rangers were notified. Zach Taylor and his goons loitered on their porch, expecting company, when Ricky arrived. Camp Tallawanda turned into a scene from an old Western showdown: the shouting from the spectators, the seventh grade posse riding in hot, and the eighth grade villains sitting and waiting for them to show up. The only thing missing was a tumbleweed rolling across the street.

"Well, look who it is," Zach stared down Ricky from his chair. "I guess you found—"

Except there was no monologue, no showdown speech, Ricky ran right up the porch and pushed Zach Taylor out of his lounge chair while he was in mid-sentence.

The scrum only lasted for a minute or two. With so many witnesses and young tattletales, the camp rangers weren't far behind. Heath, Chuck, and several camp rangers broke up the bedlam. No one was severely injured, just a few flailing punches and pushing and shoving. However, Patrick once again managed to get himself a bloody nose. After they separated the two sides, and took the story from several witnesses, Heath and Chuck drove two golf carts to take Ricky, Zach, Nolan, and Patrick to report immediately to Commissioner Powell. The speculators convinced the crowd of rubberneckers all four of them surely would be going home.

* * *

Ricky sat in the reception room on the couch next to Heath, then Chuck, Patrick, Nolan, and Zach at the other end. The boys' shirts were ruffled or ripped, and they had scraped knees from the tussle. Margaret played solitaire on the computer.

"I can sense the tension in the room," Margaret said. "Looks like you boys got yourselves into quite the dust-up out there, didn't you?"

Nobody answered.

"It's a shame," she winked at Ricky. "I'd hate to have to send that cute face home early."

A few more minutes went by with nothing said. Margaret provided the only sound in the room, clicking the buttons on her keyboard, and occasionally swigging from an empty soda cup. She'd slurp, then give the ice a quick shake with one hand, and slurp again. An instant before the phone rang, she slammed down on it and picked it up in midair.

"Yes sir," she said and hung up.

"He's ready. Doesn't sound too happy either," she slurped some more and pointed with turquois nails to the door.

Commissioner Powell sat facing the window, his back to the entrance of the room. A cloud of smoke surrounded his shadow. He rocked in his chair about a millimeter back and fourth.

"Get in here and shut the dang door," he grunted.

They hurried to take their seats, like musical chairs, nobody wanted to sit down last, and it was Patrick who got stuck standing. All six of them equally confused how it was possible, but somehow, sitting right there on Powell's desk was Ricky's mangled wooden stick.

"I've been overseeing this camp since before any of you were born," Commissioner Powell began, still sitting with his back to the group, and puffing his cherry pipe. "I've seen hundreds of pranks in my day, some of them good, most of them lacking in creativity, and a few of them despicable. I know that's a part of the camp life here at Tallawanda. But I have never seen the down right malicious, vile theft and conversion of another's property like we have sitting in front of us today."

Ricky started to think that maybe he was in the clear, and that it was just going to be the eighth graders getting sent home. The tension around his heart loosened. He could feel his shoulders straightening out.

"But this camp has a strict zero tolerance policy for violence. You can't go around fighting at this camp. You can't cause mayhem."

Maybe not, Ricky thought tensing up all over again.

Commissioner Powell turned around slowly. It was a maneuver that he probably hoped would have been smoother, because he had to use his feet to rotate his large body in the rocking chair. It took him several hard attempts as his body reeled awkwardly trying to lunge his weight around until he faced his visitors head-on. They wanted to, but no one dared laugh.

"Look at you," he huffed.

He put his pipe down and reached into his drawer for sunflower seeds, popping a fistful into his mouth. Then he took of his sunglasses. Despite the darkness in the room, his tiny pupils showed off his gazing blue eyes.

"I ought to send all of you home," he stuck his tongue between his teeth and sucked while rotating his lower jaw to spit out some seeds. "I really ought to."

He let the words hang in the air and inspected the object that started the fight.

"It's a shame," Powell shook his head while running his hands over the stick. "Truly an act of war, young man," he said with a soul-piercing gaze into Zach's eyes. "But," he raised a finger and shifted his glare to Ricky, "That gives you no right to go off causing a riot. Not at my camp!"

Powell slammed his fist on the table.

"I know it wasn't just you four either. It was your whole cabins," Commissioner Powell hardly stopped to take a breath. "And quite frankly, I need to put a stop to it. I let it slide the first time I heard about it on the lacrosse field. Now? I get an all out backyard brawl. What would your parents say, Mr. Collins? And what about you, Patrick Winkerton? You want to be the first member of your family forcibly removed from Camp Tallawanda?"

Patrick started to sniffle, and then tears rushed down his face.

"Stop crying!" Commissioner Powell commanded. "Yes, you are all equally guilty as far as I see it, and there needs to be a punishment. I can't appear to look soft in my old age. Camp Tallawanda is a place of character, and learning, and I won't allow anarchy here."

Powell picked up the ugly trophy once again.

"Mr. Taylor?" he asked.

"Sir?"

"Did you learn anything about these sticks before you decided to desecrate this one here?"

Zach nodded yes. But Powell started talking without caring much about his answer. "Back in the history of this land, before the European settlers, the First Nation played the game of lacrosse."

Zach and the others nodded, they remembered the video from crafts class.

"In some cultures, it was called 'Little War.' Two battling tribes would come together and play the game. The winner taking all the spoils. Ranger Gladys taught you that, didn't see?"

"Yes, Sir," Zach said.

"And did she teach you that a man's stick was a part of him, Mr. Taylor? That is was sacred?" Powell held the trophy of Ricky's destroyed stick for Zach to look at.

Zach hesitated, "Yes, Sir."

"Well, I don't think you learned it. So, I'm going to teach it to you again. You rascals want to battle each other? Somebody has to get sent home. I'll settle this the way the first players of this game would have it settled it. And it just so happens, you're all in luck. We had a cancellation of our main attraction for parents weekend coming up."

Commissioner Powell reached towards his intercom to ask Margaret for something, but before he could get his hand over to the button, her voice came on over the speaker, "Yes, Sir?"

"Margaret," Commissioner Powell spoke into the intercom. "Did we ever get confirmation for the carnival for parents weekend?"

"No sir, they cancelled on us," Margaret answered, chomping her gum. "Something about some lost paperwork, sir."

"Yes, I knew that, but did you ever find out what paperwork exactly was missing?" Powell shook his head.

"No, sir. In fact, I couldn't find any paperwork," Margaret reported.

"So, do we have a main event for the parents on Sunday?" Powell clarified.

"No sir, not yet."

"Very good," Commissioner Powell smiled. "I have an idea."

Powell turned off his intercom and rocked in his chair, looking back at the worried boys in his office.

"I ought to send all of you—and your whole cabins for that matter—outta here right now. But instead, next weekend, Parents Weekend, on Sunday at high noon, in front of all of Camp Tallawanda's campers and parents, Salamander cabin will play Porcupine cabin in a lacrosse game. The whole ordeal: referees, scoreboard, game clock, bleacher seats, free concession stands, games for the kids, the works! I want every camper and parent in attendance. Chuck and Heath here, you'll coach. The winning cabin will get this trophy, and the losing team will be dismissed from camp immediately for violating camp rules," Powell slammed his fist on his desk. "And that's final."

CHAPTER 27

That's What Friends Do

Word about the game spread like wildfire throughout the camp. Ricky's parents received a personal handwritten letter from Commissioner Powell. Powell crafted the letter with such shrewd language, that whatever he said in there, Ricky's parents weren't too upset with him for 'defending his honor against extreme and outrageous conduct.' Ricky's mother of course, hoped he'd lose the game so that Ricky could come home early.

Claire knew all about the Big Game against Porcupine before Ricky said anything to her. She shoulder tapped him with her normal stick in the cafeteria and after dinner, they played catch at Cooke Field under the lights. Claire told Ricky she felt terrible Zach ruined his stick, and she thought Ricky was brave but also an idiot for running up to Porcupine cabin and shoving Zach Taylor to the ground.

She thinks I'm brave, he smiled, *I am brave.* Claire's blonde curls sparkled under the field lights. Her loose sweatshirt kept away the mosquitoes. Then, Ricky told her about what happened to the guys at the lake with the eighth grade girls.

"You probably would have been there too, you know," she reminded him.

"Well, I was hoping it would have been me and you going to the lake," Ricky said showing his courage. He threw the ball a little high on purpose so Claire would have to run after it, but she reached out with one hand on her stick and somehow caught it anyways.

"Yea right," she said, and threw it back hard and fast. "I'm sure going to miss you next week."

"Hey, come on. Do you think we got a chance against them?"

"It doesn't matter what anyone thinks, only matters what you do. I'm excited to watch. Are you going to score a goal for me?"

"One for you, and two for me," Ricky threw a perfect left-handed pass.

"No chance you'll get a hat-trick. But, you better score one for me."

"What do I get if I do?" Ricky blushed.

"I'll get my slow dance you promised me, that's what," she said.

"And what if I don't?"

"If you don't score any goals, your whole team is probably going home," Claire belted another hard pass directly into Ricky's pocket.

"If I get a hat-trick, then you're meeting me at the lake," Ricky said throwing it back a little harder too, but right on target.

"If I were you, I'd worry more about winning the game and less about scoring goals," Claire advised.

"Well then if we win, will you meet me at the lake?"

"Maybe," she threw one way over Ricky's head on purpose.

* * *

It was late Saturday night, the night before the Little War Game, and the boys were laughing about the day's activities with everyone's parents.

"Ricky's parents take the cake," Ace's voice said in the dark, and everyone in the cabin laughed in unison.

"Nobody's going to argue that one," Marcus chuckled. "Ricky how do you handle it?"

"Surprised you're normal," Dane admitted. "If mine were so strict like that, I'd prob be a total weirdo."

"You are weird, Dane," Spencer snapped out as fast as he could, which caused a pillow to go flying across the room in his direction.

Ricky laughed along with everyone else.

"Hey, Dez's mom's the one who said she hoped we loose and go home early," Artie reminded everyone.

"Oh so what?" Dez scoffed. "Everyone's mom said that."

"Yeah, but Ricky's mom asked if he could go home even if we win," Ben Li chimed in.

Ben's insult reminded Ricky and the rest of the cabin just how high the stakes were for their big game tomorrow. Ricky tried to apologize to everyone for what he'd gotten them into.

"Don't worry about it," Artie said to Ricky. "I think this is the best thing ever."

"Yeah, seriously, Ricky," TJ echoed. "This will be the biggest crowd we've ever played in front of."

"Plus," Marcus added. "It's not like you were the only one who went over there and started that fight. Well, you started it. But, we all joined in."

"Yeah, but I could have cost us the rest of our summer," Ricky worried.

"Hey, we knew what we were doing; we wanted to back you up," TJ said. "That's what friends do."

"Really? The way you guys been making fun of me all summer, I wasn't sure if I was your friend."

"Ricky, partner? Are you crazy?" Ace asked kicking up at Ricky from the bottom bunk.

"Dude, we make fun of everybody," Great Dane explained.

"Yeah man," TJ continued, "why would you think you aren't our friend?"

"Cause all you guys do is make fun of me," Ricky did his best to not let his voice crack. "And you keep saying I was the one who peed the bed."

"Ricky, is there anyone in this cabin who doesn't get made fun of?" Marcus asked.

Ricky paused, he'd never thought about it like that, "I guess not," he admitted.

"Don't you get it?" Dez explained. "You're the new guy, so we give you a little extra hard time, but that's what we did to Ace last year."

"Man, I'll tell you what; you need to lighten up," Ace explained. "A'course you're cool."

"I am?" Ricky laughed.

"Barely," Spencer answered.

"See, Ricky? That's how friends talk to each other," TJ went on. "And we all know Spencer is the one who pissed the bed."

"Then why don't you guys make fun of him for it?" Ricky asked.

"Cause it don't bother him," Dane explained. "You get all worked up. It's more fun teasing you."

"So, I'm just not supposed to let it bother me?" The light bulb went off in his head. Suddenly, the entire summer started to make sense. *These guys make fun of each other all the time. But they're all best friends.*

"That's not what my friends did at my old town," Ricky explained.

"Ricky, did you ever hang out with your friends in your old town?" TJ cut to the chase.

"Not really," Ricky confessed.

"Well, that's what friends do: they make each other laugh and they laugh at each other," TJ told him.

"Hey Ricky," Marcus chimed in. "You know what else friends do?"

"No. What?" he answered.

"They pass the ball!" Marcus groaned in the dark.

"Yeah!" the entire cabin repeated.

"Well, I never passed it to anyone cause I wanted you guys to see how much better I got."

"Ricky, no one will ever admit that you're good. But you still have to pass the ball," Dez said. "You gotta be a good team player."

"Speaking of," Heath's voice interrupted the team bonding session. "Why don't you guys get some sleep? We have a big day tomorrow."

"We have to win," Ricky told them, for the first time feeling like part of the 'we.'

"Yeah guys," said TJ. "We have a victory party to go to tomorrow night"

The boys cheered in the dark.

"Spencer?" asked Ricky once there was lull in the cheering.

"Yeah?"

"You know you're not supposed to let shots go into the net, right?" Ricky laughed. His first real insult of the summer was met with raucous cheers.

"Oh shut up," Spencer finally said over the yelling. "Hey Artie? Why don't you try getting in the game? And Ace, how about you win a face-off against Zach Taylor for once in your life?"

"Hey partner, I got nothin' to do with this, don't be draggin' me in here for no reason."

"Heath," Ben Li asked.

"Yeah, Ben?"

"Do you think we're going to win tomorrow?"

The question brought total silence to the room.

Heath cleared his throat, "Well, the eighth graders are a year older than you guys. They're a little bigger, a little stronger, and a little faster, and some of them are pretty darn good. But you guys practiced all summer and they haven't. So, that means you have an extra season of work on them. Hard work beats talent when talent doesn't work hard."

"But do you think we're going to win?" Ben asked again.

"I *know* you'll win tomorrow," Heath paused for the dramatic effect. "You have a better coach."

This brought shouts, boos, laughs and pillows from all angles tossed at Heath.

CHAPTER 28

Suiting Up, Warming Up

Packing was not easy. Finding clothes that had been borrowed, stolen, or lost in the laundry took some time. They found missing socks, and underwear, and of course, jerseys and pads that couldn't be forgotten. The camp supplied each boy with a large canvas bag to throw their dirty clothes in after the game, and another bag to return any lacrosse equipment that belonged to the camp. After the game, they'd have enough time to shower, but the losers would have to leave before dinner with their parents.

Knock. Knock.

"Guys, someone is here," Artie shouted looking out the window. "I think it's TJ's dad."

"It is," TJ confirmed. "Open the door."

"Hey guys," said Mr. Stanton holding a big box in his hand.

Mr. Stanton stood about 6'3" with a long torso, skinny legs, and a spare tire around his waist. He looked exactly like an older and greyer version of TJ. They even had the same haircut.

"TJ told me the last time you guys played the eighth graders, they wore their junior high school jerseys, and you guys were all mismatched. So," he dropped the box to the ground. "I thought it would be a good idea if you guys looked like a real team. TJ's uncle owns a sports store, and he had these from a botched order last year."

Mr. Stanton opened the box and held up a black lacrosse jersey. It had white and gold numbers and gold and white stripes on the sleeves. The box was full of them.

The boys marveled at the high quality jersey. It was even nicer than the junior high issued jerseys the eighth graders would be wearing. Without even touching it, the boys could see from the logo it was made from the best lightweight flexible material, the same kind college and pro teams wear. The campers swarmed the box.

"Thank you Mr. Stanton," Heath said. "You didn't have to do that, sir.

"It was nothing," Mr. Stanton waived off the compliment. "My brother-in-law says they were just collecting dust."

"Dibs on number one," TJ called.

"Shoot, then I gotta get eleven," Ace reasoned. "Like blackjack."

This lead to a barrage of number requests and explanations based on what was in the box: Marcus claimed number 7 for good luck, Great Dane took 99 because it was the biggest, Dez grabbed 28 to match his birthday, and so on. All the while, the boys oohed and ahhed about how cool the black and yellow jerseys looked as they rummaged around to find the numbers they wanted. Ricky got lucky, lying at the bottom of the box was the number 45 jersey; it matched his dinosaur practice pinnie.

"Well, I'm glad you guys like them," Mr. Stanton said. "Good luck today, see ya TJ." He hugged his son.

"Thanks Dad."

"Thanks Mr. Stanton!"

"Thanks TJ's dad."

"Thanks," the rest of the cabin added in.

After Mr. Stanton left, they spent a few more minutes admiring the new jerseys. Every boy wearing black and gold brought a sense of unity over the cabin. They no longer looked like a band of organized misfits; each cabin member admired his neighbor, his teammate. The entire feeling of the room focused itself on the task at hand. But first, they'd need to finish packing.

"Is everyone's bags ready to go?" Heath asked.

The boys had their beds made and their trunks emptied. Salamander was as close to clean as a seventh grade boys' summer cabin could get. The lingering sounds of zipped-up luggage broke the silent void. A sense of uneasiness lingered in the room. Was this their last day of camp?

"Guys, you won't win unless you believe you're going to win," Heath explained. "Everyone is standing here packed up and prepared to leave for the summer. I'm not ready to leave yet. Are you guys ready to leave? Are you guys ready to go home and get back to school? Or do you want to stay at Camp Tallawanda!"

"Stay!" they shouted.

Heath ripped the covers off his freshly made bed and dumped all the contents of his duffle bag on top of it. Spencer's eyebrows rose to his hairline in surprise. Open-mouthed they wondered to each other if their leader had lost his mind.

"If you plan to lose, you're going to lose. Everybody dump your bags out, we aren't going anywhere," Heath announced. "Mess up your beds!"

The boys exchanged smiles, shouting in excitement, they ripped the covers off their beds, and tipped their bags upside down spilling clothes around the cabin. They set their minds to stay at Camp Tallawanda. They had to stay.

* * *

The whole camp and everyone's parents made their way to Cooke Field to watch the Little War Game, as they called it. There must have been at least five or six hundred people, but for the boys who had to play in front of the crowd, it felt like 10,000. The camp even set up bleacher seating. Commissioner Powell ordered in several food trucks to serve as the concession stands. They offered hot dogs, burgers, cotton candy, and all the other tailgating classics for everyone in attendance. Nobody had to pay for anything.

Margaret worked the scoreboard, which counted down 30 minutes until game time. Right there on the table next to Margaret, rested Ricky's broken lacrosse stick. Dunked in shiny gold plastic and screwed into a wooden plaque, that's what they were playing for. Someone inscribed the words *'The Little War Trophy'* into its wooden plaque. The winners would receive a mangled trophy, and the right to stay at camp.

"Look at that over there," Ricky pointed at the trophy as they walked across the field to their bench. "That's mine, and we're getting it back."

Camp Ranger Steepdun's voice could be heard all over the field coming out of the speakers, "Lady's and Gentleman, parents, and *kempers*, boys and girls, we've got ourselves a be-ute-afill day for lacrosse. The current temperature on the field is a perfect 28 degrees Celsius, with a light 5 kilometer per hour breeze. We're in for a real treat today mates."

Clad in their junior high issued blue and white game jerseys, the Porcupine cabin took the field. They had matching gloves, helmets and cleats, and expected to force the Salamander cabin to wear their hodgepodge of reversible white practice pinnies. However, when the Salamanders entered in matching black and gold jerseys, the eighth graders stopped to stare. Although the seventh graders looked a little sloppy with mismatching helmets and shorts, their jerseys were brand new and obviously better than the eighth graders'. The boys from Porcupine began questioning their jerseys and suddenly didn't feel so superior.

Patrick Winkerton pointed at them and whined, "How come they get brand new jerseys?"

"You see that guys?" Heath asked as they strolled onto their end of the field. "They're looking at us. The game's already started and we're in the lead. Look good, feel good, play good. Now let's start to warm up like we know what we're doing over here."

Heath picked up the pace, and the Salamanders followed behind him. The team ran a warm-up lap around their half of the field, then filed into lines to stretch. Heath took Spencer over into the goal for practice shots.

"And what's with you?" Heath asked Spencer. "Aren't you hot wearing those ugly sweat pants?"

"No," Spencer shrugged, looking at his multi-color designed jogging pants.

"Take those off, you look like a clown. You'll get dehydrated," Heath said.

"I can't."

"Why not? Are you hiding shin guards, or something?" Heath joked.

"Yeah," Spencer admitted casually.

"Spencer!" Heath whispered and shouted at the same time. "You're wearing shin guards? No self-respecting lacrosse goalie is supposed to wear shin guards."

"I'll respect myself after we beat the eighth graders."

"Unbelievable," Heath said taking a low shot, and Spencer kicked it away off his shin without any sign of pain or fear.

"See? It's better," Spencer explained. "It's not against the rules, is it?"

"You're a real piece of work Spencer," Heath replied.

The players' parents walked by on their way to the bleachers, some waived, others shouted good luck, but Mr. and Mrs. Collins walked right onto the field to talk to their son. Mrs. Collins held a sweatshirt under her arm, never one to trust the weather. Mr. Collins held a set of foam bleacher seat pads and his own light jacket his wife insisted he bring.

"This is so cool," Mrs. Collins observed.

"Where did you get all this stuff?" Mr. Collins asked, talking about the lacrosse equipment. "Did I pay for this?"

"No, the camp gave it to us. I'm just borrowing most of it."

"Do you have enough water?" Mrs. Collins asked.

Ricky waived his parents away, as the boys laughed in the background, "I'm fine, I'm fine."

"I'm so excited to see what all this lacrosse commotion is about," Mrs. Collins said. "I've been doing some research on the internet about it." Then she lowered her voice to a murmur, "Are you wearing a cup?"

"For crying out loud, Mom. Yes!"

"And you said you played middle field? Is that offense or defense?"

"It's both, Mom,"

"Be careful out there," Mrs. Collins stressed.

"Rick, get over here!" Heath called. "Let's go. We got a game to get ready for."

"Okay, son, Good luck," Mr. Collins said.

"Be careful," Mrs. Collins tried hugging him again, but Ricky wrestled her off.

He strapped on his white and chrome-masked helmet and rejoined the team in warm-ups. The guys conducted catching and passing drills. Then, they worked on getting ground balls, face-offs, and reviewed their offensive motions. Heath reminded the team that the most important thing was to keep possession of the ball.

"Don't do too much, we don't need any heroes," Heath lectured. He made sure to say it looking right at Ricky.

Ricky didn't have the luxury of actually playing a real lacrosse game before, his stomach felt like a blender with the lid left off. But it was a good feeling. This was the first time in his life, he ever played in a real sports game of any kind. The people, the referees, the scoreboard; he loved all of it. He couldn't wait for his chance to get into the game and show everybody that he wasn't just the nerdy new kid, and that he had some real athletic talent too. Ricky wondered whether his parents would be impressed or concerned at the discovery. He scanned the crowd and caught Claire walking down the sidelines with her family. Her curly sand-colored ponytail jutted out the back of her baseball cap. He whistled at her, and she turned and pointed to her hat holding up three fingers to remind him of the hat-trick.

"Romeo!" Heath called to Ricky with his hands on his hips. "Are you focused?"

"I'm focused," Ricky replied.

"Are you focused on the game?" Heath yelled back and the guys laughed. They took turns running down the lane, and passing it behind the goal to X, then the X passed it to the next guy coming across who took a shot on Spencer.

"Dane, now you?" Heath yelled towards the sidelines. Ricky turned to spot Great Dane standing at the bleachers talking to Paige and her parents.

"You guys are ridiculous," Heath groaned. "Where are your heads at?"

"We're worried about the after party," Spencer answered from standing in the goal.

The scoreboard said only 5 five more minutes until game time.

CHAPTER 29

The Little War

"Ladies an' gentleman," Steepdun's said over the loud speakers. "Please rise for the national anthem."

As the crowd rose to their feet, Mrs. Collins leaned over to Mr. Collins to say, "Look at this; they're making a whole production out of all this? I thought these boys were in trouble. I can see they're certainly learning their lesson, all right. This is quite the rigmarole for a punishment."

The players stood along the sideline during the National Anthem, holding their helmets. Unlike football and baseball, Ricky learned that in lacrosse, the team's benches were on the same side of the field, separated by the scoring table, like basketball. The eighth grade girls' cabin leader, Nicole Nensworth operated the penalty box. Ricky doubted it would be much of a penalty having to talk to her.

"I've never played a lacrosse game in front of so many people," Artie said to Ricky on the sidelines.

"I've never played a lacrosse game," Ricky laughed.

Ricky turned around one more time to give a head nod to his parents, then he searched for Claire and gave her a quick waive. *Play it cool,* he scolded himself.

Ace headed out to the middle of the field to take the opening face-off. Dez was paired up once again with Patrick on the far side of the field; the two nodded but didn't say anything. Dez sniffed loudly to remind Patrick of the first 'dog breath' incident.

As Ace approached Zach Taylor at center field for the face off, Zach asked, "Ready to get sent home?"

"Not really. We ain't even pack."

"What? You were supposed to," Zach was stunned by the response.

"Don't need to pack if we ain't leaving, do we?"

The two players crouched down on the ground with the ball between their sticks waiting for the referee to blow the whistle. When he did, Zach clamped down on the ball quickly, and rotated his body, knocking Ace on his side. Zach had won another face-off.

"Aaaannnd we're off," Steepdun announced.

Ace had to sprint to catch up with Zach. He gave him a few useless whacks on the shoulders. Zach ran the ball down and got it into the offensive zone easily, and passed it to the attackman.

"Not the best start," Artie commented to Ricky on the sidelines.

"Ball is up top," Spencer shouted from the goal, as the attackman ran behind him and passed it to the top of the box.

"Dane slide over, slide over!" directed Spencer.

The ball got back to Zach. He held it casually down at his side, as Ben shuffled over to cover him. Zach signaled for another Porcupine midfielder to run over and set a pick on Ben.

"Watch the pick," Dane shouted. "Slide right, Slide right."

Dane ran to cover Zach, and Ben had to spin off and switch onto the picking midfielder to keep Zach from passing it back to him. Zach ran full speed down the center crease. Dane shuffled over to put a hard check on him, but Zach was too fast; he got the shot off before Dane made contact. Although Dane knocked Zach to the ground just a second after he released the shot, it was a second too late. Zach scored the first goal of the game.

The crowd cheered, the eighth graders' bench erupted, and Zach popped up off the ground yelling and mimicking a bow and arrow shot with his stick, "Taylor Phaser on the board early!"

"Man, I hate that guy," Artie kicked at the ground.

"Start packing!" Zach pumped his fist to Ace.

Heath roamed up and down the sidelines clapping to the bench, "We're fine guys, we're fine. Stay focused. Pick up your teammates. It's a long game."

"Let's go Ace," Ricky shouted. "You got this, bud. Let's go!"

On the next face-off, Zach wasn't able to win it so cleanly. Zack and Ace wrestled at the centerline, which and brought over the other midfielders for an all out groundball scrum. Ben Li stuck his face right into the mess of players, and emerged with the ball. He sprinted down to the offensive zone. Ben tried to throw it to Dez, but Patrick swatted the ball out of mid-air and sprinted off with it in the opposite direction. But, when Patrick crossed over the centerline, the referee blew the whistle for an offsides penalty.

"That was lucky," Heath smiled to the sidelines.

"Cheaters!" Spencer heckled.

"Offsides?" Mrs. Collins leaned over to her husband for clarification. "What is offsides?"

Mr. Collins had already reached into his back pocket and was thumbing through a copy of an official lacrosse rulebook. "Says here, you cannot have more than six men on the offensive half of the field. So now Ricky's team will get possession of the ball."

"Run the offense," Heath reminded them from the sidelines.

Ace passed the ball down to Marcus, and then ran into the center crease. Marcus passed the ball back up to Ben who ran across from left to right. The defender on Ace moved over to cover Ben, so Ben threw the ball down to the crease where Ace was wide open. Nolan and the defense were so concentrated on Ace being wide-open, they didn't notice Marcus coming around from behind the goal. Ace made a quick pass. The ball entered and left Marcus's stick almost instantly, and hit the back of the net.

"Gooooaaaaallll!" Steepdun shouted over the cheering crowd.

The seventh grader bench erupted in simultaneous joy. Everyone lifted their hands to the air, then high-fived their neighbors. Marcus accepted his congratulations from his teammates on the field. Ace jogged off, signaling for Ricky to fill-in.

"Go Ricky!" Claire shouted from the crowd.

"Did you hear that?" Mrs. Collins asked her husband. "There's some girl cheering for Ricky. No wonder why he wanted to go to that dance."

"Right now, I'm more concerned about someone whacking him with one those sticks out there," Mr. Collins replied.

Ricky lined up to take the face off against Zach Taylor.

"Trying to get your stick back, huh?" Zach asked him.

"I'll send you a postcard from camp," Ricky responded getting down in face-off position.

The ref blew the whistle to start the play, but before he did, Ricky anticipated it, and his timing was perfect. Ricky clamped down on the ball before Zach. He actually won the face-off. He shoveled the ball forward and scooped it in stride. Ricky sprinted down the field thinking about nothing else other than scoring a goal. Two defenders closed in on him from both sides, trying to stop Ricky from getting a clean lane into the crease, which left Marcus wide open.

Everything Ricky learned that summer about lacrosse told him to pass it to Marcus, but how cool would it be to take the faceoff and run it down and score a solo goal? In a half second he made up his mind and took the shot. Nolan made an easy save.

"Dang it, Ricky!" Heath barked from the sidelines.

"Come on, dude!" Marcus screamed as he chased down the defender to cover the clear. "I was wide open man!"

Since Ricky ran down the field and shot so quickly, the chasing defenders were in perfect position for a clear in the opposite direct. Nolan made on quick pass and the ball was back into the seventh grade zone. Before the Salamanders could recover properly on defense, the Porcupines had scored again.

"Oh the fireworks continue on the field, folks!" Steepdun commented over the crowd.

"Keep working the ball around guys. Don't play selfish," Heath encouraged the players after the goal, everyone knew the last part was meant for Ricky.

Ricky stayed on the field, but Zach went off for a breather. Ricky won another face-off. This time, Ricky made sure to pass the ball down to Marcus. Marcus was still frustrated, so instead of moving the offense, he took a long distance shot that soared high over the goal. Luckily, Dez was behind the goal at X, so the Salamanders kept possession.

"You guys are letting them get too many shots!" Chuck yelled at the eighth graders on the sidelines.

Dez put the ball in play from behind the goal, and passed it to Marcus on the right. Marcus passed it up to Ben Li, who fed it to the opposite side back to Dez. Dez turned and took a quick shot, but Nolan was able to make the save again.

"Clear, clear," Nolan yelled as he ran the ball out from the goal.

"Get a ride!" Heath ordered from the sidelines. Heath was making sure every player aligned with their man to man responsibility.

Nolan attempted a pass to Patrick Winkerton, but he dropped the ball, which lead to another scrum. Three or four players from each team chased the ball around kicking it across the field. They hacked at each other, trying to prevent anyone from picking it up.

"Oh my," Mrs. Collins gasped from the bleachers. "Doesn't that hurt?" she asked her husband.

One of the referees called a penalty on Ben Li for pushing someone in the back near the groundball. Zach subbed back into the game, and Ace came in for Ricky. When Ricky walked over to his water bottle with his tail between his legs, too embarrassed to look up to Claire. He knew she'd be disappointed in his selfish shot.

The seventh graders had to play a man down for thirty seconds. Zach started with the ball after the penalty. He sprinted hard to the goal. TJ put his whole body on him trying to knock him off his course, but Zach kept driving. The eighth grader from the top left crashed in and Zach faked the pass to him, and then took a hard shot.

Spencer extended his leg all the way out and across in the nick of time. The ball bounced off Spencer's hidden shin guards and rolled far up out of the zone. The crowd cringed imagining how much the save must have hurt the young goalie. Unfortunately, the Porcupines sprinted to the loose ball first, and maintained possession.

"Nice save, Spencer," Ricky and the rest of the sidelines shouted to him.

"Oooh right of the leg there!" Steepdun winced from the microphone. "That's Spencer Lutz at goalkeeper for the Salamander *kabeen*. Great stuff Goalie, good on you!"

"Ricky, when Ben Li gets released to go back in after this penalty, I want you to sub in for Ace; he's tired already," Heath said with his hand on Ricky's shoulder pad. "I want to catch these guys in transition okay?"

Ricky nodded.

"Hey Rick," Heath placed a hand on Ricky's helmet. "Don't be selfish."

"Release!" Nicole yelled and Ben Li ran back on to the field.

"Coming on!" Chuck pointed to his guys on the field. "Coming on!"

As Ben Li rushed the field, it forced the eighth grade attackman to take a selfish shot, and Spencer caught it cleanly in his stick.

"Cleeeaarr!" Spencer called to the team, telling them to spread out and get down the field.

Ace sprinted with whatever he had left in his tank towards the sidelines, tapping his stick on his head signaling he needed a sub.

"Ricky get ready... go!"

As soon as Ace stepped one foot over the line, Ricky took off sprinting into the center of field. No one was there to cover him. Spencer hit Ricky with a laser pass that Ricky caught in stride and continued sprinting straight to the goal uncovered.

"Slide over," Nolan commanded the defenders who were nowhere near the center of the field. Ricky barreled down at a full sprint. This time he truly was wide open. He let out a rocket shot that ripped past Nolan's shoulder and kicked out the back of the net for all the fans to see.

"Ricky sored a goal!" Mrs. Collins jumped up and down and hugged Mr. Collins. "He scored a goal! I can't believe it." Then she turned her attention to the field "Yay Ricky! Be careful, honey!"

"Way to go, son!" Mr. Collins shouted over the cheering fans.

Ricky looked to the stands to see his parents, then he found Claire, and he raised one finger in the air. She raised two back at him.

"Gooooaaaaallll!" Steepdun roared. "And we've got the seventh graders from Salamander *kabeen* tied with the eighth grade Porcupine *kabeen* two to two. Great stuff here, mates. Great stuff."

* * *

After Ricky's goal, the game got sloppy for the rest of the first quarter. There were lots of ground balls, missed passes and minimal action. At one point though, Zach hit Artie so hard that Artie dropped his stick and the ball he had in it. The whole eighth grade bench shouted, "Yard Sale." But no one else scored; the first quarter ended 2-2.

At the end of the first quarter, the team gathered around Heath for a quick time-out.

"Hey hey, one down, three quarters to go. You guys are doing awesome," Heath clapped. "The biggest thing right now is that we need to cover up the ground balls. Don't be afraid to get your head down, and pick up the ground balls, guys. It's not field hockey!"

Over on the other bench, Chuck's veins bulged out of his neck and forehead.

"We're getting embarrassed out here!" Chuck screamed. "Do you guys want to go home for the summer? If you keep playing like this you're going home! Make plays," he roared. "Make plays!"

The second quarter started with Porcupine winning another faceoff. An eighth grade attackman weaved, dipped, and dove past what seemed like every seventh grader on the field. Then, he scored with a sidearm bounce shot that hit off the side pipe and into the goal. The eighth graders scored two more in a row after that, and had the lead 5-2. On the last possession of the first half of the game, the seventh graders got the ball into the offensive zone, and Heath called a time-out. When they gathered on the sidelines, they expected him to have a play drawn up.

Heath took the clipboard out and he drew two O's out in front of the goal. He started to explain all sorts of movements and what he wanted everyone to do, but nothing Heath was saying made any sense. The boys started laughing when the play that he was drawing starting to look like a fat guy with a mustache.

"Look guys," Heath put the clipboard down. "Just run the offense, don't be selfish, wait for the true shot, and let's get one more before halftime, okay? Have fun."

Heath's advice relieved the pressure. The seventh graders jogged onto the field feeling loose. Heath instructed Dez to start with the ball at the top, knowing this would bring a middie on him instead of the usual long stick defender. This simple maneuver left the small and shifty Dez with more space to work. He ran down to the left, passed to Ben; Ben gave a great fake pass back to Dez, but instead threw it around to Marcus. Marcus managed to pass it right back to Ben, who was practically standing in the goal. Ben raised his stick up high with both hands, which caused Nolan to lift his stick for the block, then Ben shot straight down, bouncing the ball into the goal. The Salamanders went into halftime losing 5-3.

CHAPTER 30

The Second Half

At halftime, even from across the field, the seventh graders could hear Chuck. They couldn't quite make out what he was saying, but they could see him pacing back and fourth throwing his arms up in the air. He pointed at various kids while yelling directly at them. At one point he threw his clipboard down in disgust.

Heath sat with his legs stretched straight out in front of him.

"This is well cut grass," he said rubbing his hand through it. He took a deep breath in through his nose. "Is there anything better than fresh cut grass? Who was on the grounds crew for this game?"

This is the halftime speech? Ricky, and most of the others, thought to themselves.

"Hey listen, TJ," Heath went on. "I'm making it your responsibility to find out who was the grounds crew for today, and tomorrow we're all going to go tell them what a good job they did out here, okay?"

Everybody laughed.

"Do any of you guys have any questions for me about the game?" Heath asked. "Cause, I don't have much to say. You're doing great. Remember, don't play selfish, and don't take bad shots. We stay or leave as a whole cabin, as a whole team."

After looking around and exchanging smiles and shrugs, no one had anything to ask.

"Ricky," Heath said. "Maybe you want to apologize for taking that terrible shot?" Health chuckled, so did everybody else, even Ricky.

"I got a question," Spencer said. "What do you guys think about these bad boys?"

Spencer stood up and dropped his ugly windbreaker sweatpants down to reveal that he actually wasn't wearing soccer shin guards as expected. He was wearing full the shin and kneepad combos of a baseball catcher, and football thigh pads. The team rolled around the ground cracking up. Only Spencer Lutz would break the unwritten rule that goalies were supposed to be tough, and weren't supposed to wear shin guards. Spencer shamelessly admitted that every inch of his lower body was covered in pads, and the whole team laughed with him.

* * *

The third quarter would be remembered as one of the single most exciting quarters of lacrosse any of the Salamander boys ever played. The teams went back and fourth trading goals, big stops, highlight caliber saves by both goalies, and phenomenal defense. Ricky scored a left-handed goal. Zach Taylor scored twice, earning a hat-trick, and Dez scored with a behind the back shot as he fell backwards. The black and gold, and blue and white jerseys scrambled all over the field, each of them determined to stay at camp.

The best play of the third quarter, no doubt, had to be when TJ Stanton intercepted a pass and sprinted down the field on offense. Once he got into the eighth grade zone, someone smacked the ball out of TJ's stick and it rolled towards the goal. TJ chased after the ball, but instead of trying to scoop it up, he lunged forward, completely horizontal, and swung at the ball almost like he was golfing. From midair, TJ managed to score a tying goal to put the game at 7-7. When the third quarter ended, it was a tie game with a score of 9-9.

* * *

"Guys this is awesome," Heath said to the team huddle during the break before the fourth quarter. "Look at this, you are ten minutes away from sending the eighth graders home early for the summer. I'm so proud of you guys, right now. Let's finish it, okay? Let's finish it. *Finish* on three 1–2–3!"

"FINISH!" the team shouted.

Porcupine started with the ball, but when the attackman at the X position tried to run around the goal into the front of the crease, Great Dane was right there. In a perfectly legal hit, Dane had his two hands together at the center of his long pole, he set a wide base with his feet, and he absolutely leveled the kid. Both of the attack's feet kicked straight out from under him about three feet in the air. He dropped to the ground straight on his back. Not only did he let go of his stick, but one of his gloves went flying off his hands too.

"OHHH!" The entire crowd recoiled. Steepdun said it on the microphone, the seventh graders shouted it on the sidelines. But the only people who weren't cheering after the hit were the eighth graders, and the boy's parents in the stands.

"Is he dead?" Mrs. Collins cried.

"Hun, stop it," Mr. Collins shushed her. "He's fine, it was a clean hit, just great timing, that's all."

"Oh, I'm so glad that wasn't Ricky," she responded.

There was nothing illegal about the hit; the refs discussed it, but didn't call a penalty. The boy got up, eventually not seriously injured, but had the wind knocked out of him. Everyone on both benches knew that with that hit, Dane set the tone for the fourth quarter.

The Salamanders started to settle into their motion triangle offense, just like Heath coached. But nobody could score. The goalies from both teams played out of their minds in the fourth quarter. It didn't matter what they did, or how they did it, both Spencer and Nolan stopped every shot that came at them.

With only one minute left in the game, it the scoreboard still read 9 to 9.

Ricky looked over to see Claire from the sidelines. Her knees bounced nervously in the bleachers and she had her hands pressed tightly together against her mouth. When she saw Ricky looking at her she stopped bouncing for a second and smiled. The seventh graders had possession of the ball after a time out, and Heath needed to sub Ricky into the game.

"Ricky," Heath yelled. "It's your stick to win. Get in there. Look, there's a minute left, okay? Wait for a good shot, alright?"

Ricky jogged on the field. There was nothing he wanted to do more than get a third goal, score a hat-trick, and be the hero of the game. Heck, it was his stick on the line, who else deserved it more than him? He wanted to prove to his new friends and his parents, and Claire, and everyone else watching that he was good at lacrosse. He wanted to win the trophy, *his* trophy. He wanted to be the hero.

"Ricky," Heath called after him, as if he could read his mind. Ricky spun around to face his cabin leader.

"It's a team sport, Ricky."

Ricky took a deep breath and nodded.

With the ball in his hands, the crowd rose to their feet for the final minute. Ricky's chest started to wrench up. Zach approached Ricky to guard him one-on-one. When the ref blew the whistle, Zach lurched at Ricky faster than he expected. Ricky tried to spin and turn his stick but Zach pushed him back causing Ricky to lose his footing. Zach gave him a violent whack on the wrist and the ball popped to the ground. Ricky and Zach swiped at each other's sticks trying to pick it up. Ricky couldn't turn the ball over, not at the end of the game. He put his face low to the ground, risking getting banged on the head or the back, bent his knees like Heath taught him, and picked up the ground ball as Zach swatted ruthlessly at his arms and wrists. Ricky ran it back to the top of the box out of harm's way.

Mrs. Collins shrieked, and rubbed her hands together. Mr. Collins put his hands on his wife's shoulders in relief. Claire removed her hat and clenched it over her face.

Ricky passed the ball to Ace, then ran to the crease to run the offense for one more try. Ace passed it to Marcus. Marcus tried to make a move to the goal but Patrick boxed him out, so he had to throw it back up to Ben Li at the top of the crease.

"Thirty seconds, left!" Margaret yelled from the scoreboard.

"Thirty seconds!" Both sidelines shouted.

Ben held the ball trying to get his defender to come after him, but the defender stood his ground.

"Come on guys," Heath snapped. "Run the offense, get a good look!"

Ben passed it back to Ricky. Zach was all over him. He couldn't go anywhere with the ball, so he threw it into the crease towards Ace.

"Twenty seconds!" Margaret shouted

"We need to get a stop," Chuck shrieked to the eighth graders. "Twenty seconds! We need to get the ball back!"

Ricky darted toward to goal, "Ace, Ace here!" He shook his stick calling for the pass. Ace passed it to him cleanly and Ricky wound up and cranked one. This was it, this was his chance, he was going to score the game-winning goal and be the hero.

But, it sailed too high.

Ricky's shot missed too high, about a foot over the net, and flew out of bounds. Dez, doing his job, was standing behind the goal at X, which meant the seventh graders would keep possession.

"Time out!" Heath yelled to the refs.

There was 15 seconds left on the clock.

"Ladies and Gentleman, what a game we have here, stay on your feet and cheer for this finale," Steepdun pressed the audience.

The spectators obeyed. The roaring applause echoed on the field louder than it had been all day. The nerves kicked in on both sidelines.

The team huddled around Heath and his clipboard.

"Alright guys, this is it." Heath said. "We gotta put one in right here. I just want to tell you guys that win or lose, I'm proud of you."

"Let's go!" shouted Spencer.

A few more of them cheered.

"Here's what we need to do," Heath said pointing to the clipboard. "Dez start—"

Ricky interrupted Heath. "Guys! Since the second I moved to this town everyone's been telling me if I don't do this or that I'll be a loser!"

Heath stopped talking, and the whole team honed in on Ricky, his face was red, dripping in sweat, and his eyes burned with fire.

"They said if I don't go to camp, I'll be a loser. If I don't play lacrosse, I'll be a loser. If I don't go to the dance, I'll be a loser. Losers don't do this, losers don't do that. That's all I've heard all summer. But no one's told me anything about winners. Do any of you know what winners don't do?"

They stayed silent; no one dared to interrupt him.

"Do you know what winners don't do?" Ricky panted hard and wiped the sweat off his forehead. The boys waited for him to answer his own question.

"Winners don't lose," Ricky said looking each of his teammates in the eyes.

They could feel Ricky's words stir their hearts. It was as if he dumped ice water over them while he spoke. The contagious energy pumped adrenaline through their veins.

"Winners don't lose," he repeated.

He went on, "Now Marcus, start with the ball down at X; make a drive for the goal. Dez cut across right, I'll fill in down for you. Ben Li, come across to replace me. Ace, if you're open on the edge, call for the ball and charge the goal. Let's go win!"

The Salamander team roared.

"Okay guys," Heath dropped the clipboard and shrugged his shoulders. "Go win."

Marcus started with the ball down at X, and as soon as the ref blew the whistle he took a hard sprint to the goal from the left, this brought a double team from the man covering Dez. Marcus passed it to Dez in front of the net on the left side but the right defender, Patrick, jammed Dez's lane to the goal preventing him from taking a shot. Dez had to pass it to Ricky at top right. Ricky knew he could try and take the shot, but he was pretty far from the goal.

Everything went into slow motion: Ricky saw Zach Taylor rumbling over to cover him with his stick up in the air. It would be almost an impossible shot to make it through both Zach and Patrick standing between him and the goal, but there was just a little window that he could take the shot if he had to. In a split second, Ricky analyzed his options, thinking about how badly he wanted to win the game. He wanted to prove to everyone he was a winner. He wanted to fix the mess he started. He wanted the hat-trick.

"Ricky, here!" someone shouted through his thoughts.

The double team left Marcus uncovered. Marcus had his stick up high coming around the goal from the right side calling for the pass. Ricky wanted the glory of the game winning shot; he wanted to be the hero, and he wanted to stay at camp. He needed to win.

Time went back to full speed. Ricky released the ball only an instant before Zach axed down on Ricky's hands, and shouldered him to the ground. Nolan lunged from his goalie crease to cover the right corner of the goal to try and make a save.

Laying flat on the ground with Zach Taylor looming over him, Ricky watched Marcus catch his pass right on the money. And because Nolan dove so far to the edge of the goal, assuming Ricky had tried to take a wide shot, the goalie had no chance of protecting the entire other half of the net. Marcus scored with ease.

"GOOOOOOAAAALLLLLLL!" Steepdun boomed over the roaring crowed.

The seventh grade sidelines threw their sticks and gloves up into the air. Ricky bounced up from the ground and joined the rest of the guys on the field who already ran over and bear hugging Marcus as they celebrated. Ace tackled Ricky from behind.

"I thought you were gonna shoot it," Ace shouted. "Ricky man, I thought you were gonna shoot it! What a pass! What a pass!"

The refs blew the whistle with one second left on the clock. They still needed one more face-off.

Ricky took the face-off against Zach. Zach was teary eyed when they met at the center of the field. Ricky considered saying something to rub it in, but decided that the scoreboard said all he needed to say. When the ref blew the whistle, Zach clamped down on the ball but Ricky wrestled with him over it. No one could pick it up, and the final second ticked off the scoreboard.

"What an upset! The Salamanders win! Salamanders win!" Steepdun's announcement made it official. "Oh and now they're rushing the field; its pandemonium here!"

CHAPTER 31

Making Amends

The Salamanders tossed their sticks, helmets, and gloves up into the air at the sound of the final whistle. The remaining seventh graders, their parents, and all the younger campers celebrating the eighth graders' loss flooded the field. At the center of the commotion, the Salamanders high-fived and bear-hugged each other after shaking hands with the eighth graders.

Once Mr. and Mrs. Collins shuffled through the throng of people, Ricky's mother squeezed him and asked, "Oh Richard, are you hurt?"

"I'm fine, Mom," Ricky pushed away.

"Well done, son." Mr. Collins patted Ricky's shoulder pads. "This is quite the exciting sport you've discovered here."

"We're so proud of you Richard," Mrs. Collins hugged him again. "We really are proud of you. You did so good! I'm so happy you didn't get hurt."

"Amazing speech, dude!" Artie pounded Ricky's shoulders interrupting the moment with his parents.

"Go celebrate with your friends," Mr. Collins nodded. "Don't worry about us."

"We're happy for you, Richard. We'll find you in a bit," his mother hugged him again.

While Ricky made his way through the crowd, he heard a girl's voice calling his name.

"Ricky, Ricky!"

He turned around expecting to see Claire; it was Hannah Havinghurst.

Heath, who was getting a congratulatory embrace from Brittney, caught eyes with Ricky and watched to see his exchange with Hannah.

"Ricky, you played so good today," Hannah fluttered her eyes as if they'd known each other for years. She didn't bother to acknowledge this was the first time she'd ever said a word to him. "I was hoping you guys would win."

Although Heath didn't say it, Ricky could hear him thinking, "I told you so."

Ricky opened his mouth to respond when he saw Claire approaching. He closed his mouth, and without saying a word, he swim-moved around Hannah, and continued on towards Claire.

"There you are," he called to her.

"Ricky, what a game!" Claire hugged him then clapped a few times jumping up and down. "Too bad you didn't get the hat-trick though," she sneered, raising a fist to give him a gentle punch on the shoulder.

Ricky caught her wrist, "Yeah, but we won."

Staring at each other, they realized simultaneously they were holding hands. Ricky felt Claire release the pressure as she opened her fingers to let go, but Ricky held on. Claire blushed, and gently lowered her fingers to hold him back.

"So, I'll see you at the lake?" he winked.

* * *

In the midst of the joy coming from the Salamander players and their families, the eighth graders watched all of it in disbelief. Most of them still wearing their blue helmets, they walked with heads down off the field. Patrick cried like a toddler that he didn't want to go home yet. Nolan Stier's parents scolded him for breaking his stick in half on the goalpost after giving up the final score.

"So long!" Spencer gave a swaying farewell waive to a crowd of Porcupines, "We'll miss you guys."

Zach Taylor and his parents walked in the opposite direction of the eighth grade traffic, straight towards Ricky.

"Young man," Zach's father said to Ricky, ignoring Claire.

Mr. Taylor wore pink shorts and a Hawaiian shirt underneath a navy blazer. Ricky could see where Zach got his sense of fashion, and his rude social skills. "My son has something he'd like to say to you," he said nudging Zach.

"No, Dad," Zach pleaded with Mr. Taylor, his voice struggled to keep from crying.

Mr. Taylor gave a firm look to his son. Zach took his wooden lacrosse stick from his dad and turned to Ricky.

"I'm sorry me and my friends ruined your stick," Zach sniffled. Looking straight to the ground, he held out his wooden stick and offered it to Ricky, "Here, take it."

"It's okay, you can keep your stick," Ricky shook his head.

"How come?" Zach tensed up and inhaled ready to say something else.

Ricky noticed that for once his heart wasn't racing; he felt calm and confident. He looked Zach straight in the eyes and before Zach could reply he said, "Cause I won mine."

* * *

Commissioner Powell finally made his way down to the center of the field with the trophy. The crowd cleared the path but did not quiet down and continued to take pictures. Commissioner Powell planned to deliver a speech he'd rehearsed about sportsmanship and traditions, but he didn't have an adequate amount of attentive listeners from the audience. Not one to waste his words, Commissioner Powell presented the trophy to Heath. As he did, he nodded at Ricky and said, "I'm happy this trophy is going back to its rightful owner, well done."

Heath put his arm around Ricky and handed him the mangled golden trophy.

"That was one heck of a pass you made at the end there," Heath said. "And an even better swim-move," Heath elbowed. "You made the right choice. You deserve this, pal."

Ricky smiled ear to ear. He hoisted the prize over his head and everyone cheered once again, including his parents. Then he got ready to send it on to the rest of his teammates, starting first with TJ.

"Well?" TJ asked holding a palm up, waiting for Ricky to say something obvious.

"You were right about coming to Camp Tallawanda," Ricky admitted.

"Yeah, you're welcome," TJ smirked.

Ricky shook his head and gave his neighbor a gentle backhand to the chest. Both of them laughed. The two friends lifted the trophy together and howled with the crowd once more.

The End

ABOUT THE AUTHOR

Michael Dave likes jokes. He was born and raised in the suburbs of Chicago, where he lives now. He graduated from Miami University, then went on to law school and became an attorney. *Camp Tallawanda* is Michael's first novel. @realmikedave

Made in the USA
Coppell, TX
20 October 2021